CE

A fifteen year old girl's modern retelling of Shakespeare's *A Midsummer Night's Dream*

by Bridget O'Dwyer

Fresh Writers Books
PO Box 82, Uniontown OH 44685

Author: Bridget O'Dwyer

Publisher: Bill Jelen

PrePress: Fine Grains (India) Private Limited
New Delhi - India

Cover: Shannon Mattiza, 6'4 Productions

Published by: Fresh Writers Books, PO Box 82
Uniontown OH 44685

Distributed by: Independent Publishers Group

First Printing: March 2006. Printed in India

Library of Congress Control Number: 2005939078

ISBN 1-932802-94-0

About the Author

Bridget O'Dwyer is an active high school senior in Shaker Heights, Ohio. Having spent a semester in Ireland, she brings Shakespeare's A Midsummer Nights Dream to a modern setting in the small Irish town of Thurles, County Tipperary.

Bridget was a winner in the 2005 Fresh Writers Writing Program. This program encourages high school students to consider literary careers and funds a summer co-op program during which this book was created. For more information about the

Fresh Writers program, contact
Bill@FreshWritersBooks.com

Acknowledgements

For Meg for fighting for me and being my insight to boys, girls, and life; for my father for believing in fairies and for being himself, and only himself; for Eugene Dwyer for giving me a job and for Pat Dwyer for never making my job easy; for Bill Dwyer and Mary Mulhearn for taking me in and being my father and my mother; for Aisling and Grainne Dwyer for being my sisters; for Mary O'Dwyer- a truly amazing woman; for Myrna Feldman for her support and endless love and excitement; for Mr. Kelly, my tenth grade English teacher for being so enthused and always believing in me; for Thrity Umrigar, for a small but extremely influential speech; for Pat Conroy for being a cool guy, a great writer, and for showing me that not one bit of this is easy; for Al, Sam, Miriam, Mia, Kay, Laur, Jackson, and Max for being the best friends that anyone could ever ask for; for a first love; for Seymour Feldman for simply being proud; for the entire transition year class- for the laughs, the tears, and the adventures; for Thurles- if it were not for the town I would have no summers, no memories, and no happy place; and for Biddy- for the stories, the potatoes, and the name.

Extra thanks to Bill Jelen for giving me this opportunity and making me a published author before I am even an adult; for Gutenburg for designing the press; for Katie Daley for the editing help; and for anyone in the world who helped make this possible. It is truly a dream come true.

Dedication

- For my mother. She is my light, my motivation, and an endless believer in all that I do.
- For Ireland, a place I now call home.

Contents

Chapter 1

"I can't be here anymore," I said to my parents during breakfast on a Saturday morning in October. "I can't spend anymore of my life doing nothing."

Neither my mother nor my father looked up from their sections of the newspaper that they had sprawled out across the kitchen table.

"Hello?" I said getting their attention. My mother put hers down.

"What can I do for you my dearest?" she asked sarcastically as she shoved a bit of dry rye toast into her mouth.

"Do you remember how last year we talked about going to Ireland over the summer so I could meet Dad's family, but never ended up going?" I said, beginning my proposal.

"No," my mother said, recovering her face with the front page of *The New York Times*.

My father, who was obviously intrigued by my statement peaked his head over the sports section and raised an eyebrow.

"Let her talk," he said to my mother, and then looked to me to continue.

"Well I was wondering if I could possibly go for a semester." My mother placed her paper back on the table and let out a large, drastic sigh.

"It's only six months mom!" I said, pleading my case.

"What is so horrible about living here with us?" she asked sadly, as if I had offended her with my suggestion.

"Nothing!" I assured her. "I just need a change," I said looking at her with desperate eyes.

"I don't know Sarah," she said. "You're only fifteen."

"A very mature and independent fifteen, if I do say so myself," I said sternly, adjusting in my seat to appear taller.

She looked to my father. He shrugged. "I just don't know if I'm ready to be away from you for that long," she in a lonesome tone.

Thankfully my father cut in. "I think she's ready," he said. "It's not like she'd be alone." I smiled at him as my mother kicked his leg under the table. She was on the verge of serious frustration.

"I'll think about it," she said. I jumped up from the table and gave each of them a hug and a kiss on the cheek.

"I know I'm ready, you just need to learn to let go, Mom," I said walking out of the kitchen. They each returned to their reading. I poked my head back around the door.

"Convince her dad!" I mouthed, hoping he could read my lips.

"I'll take care of it," he mouthed back. I gave him a big thumbs up and ran to my room happily.

That day in October, I could only have expected another boring old afternoon wasted away by sulking in my room or whining to my parents. And then it happened. On this particular, life changing day, my parents actually agreed to consider my leaving and going to school in Ireland. I taped hits of persuasion around the house; pictures of gorgeous Irish scenery that I had printed off the internet. At dinner I further encouraged them by dramatically explaining my reasoning for wanting to leave.

"There is a world outside of Syracuse and I need to see it. I have never been anywhere and I need to experience new things. I hope you'll consider and while you're deciding, please consider my happiness and what is best for me." I quietly stood up from the table. I left the room feeling good about my heartfelt, emotional speech. I giggled at how ridiculous I had sounded but prayed it would work.

That night as I lay in bed trying to fall asleep my dad knocked on my door and sat down at the edge of my bed. He shared with me, amazing stories about his many adventures as a boy in his hometown of Thurles, County Tipperary, Ireland. He told me what it was like to live there. I could sense in his voice that he missed it while he talked about his family. It seemed as if when he told me a story he was there, re-living the moment.

"Dad," I said. "How come we've never gone over to see your family?"

"It's just been too expensive for all of us to go. It's been hard. I want you to see it and I want you to know your grandmother. It's a whole different way of life. You'd love it."

My mother overheard him sharing stories and came into my room. She sat down next to him on the bed.

"While you were dropping hits around the house today your father called your uncle Jack," she began. "Unfortunately for me, he was thrilled with the idea of you going to stay with him."

She looked sad, yet content. She faked a sniffle as if she was beginning to cry.

"You can go," she said pouting.

I shot up in my bed. "Really?" I asked in disbelief. I looked to my father; he nodded.

"Thank you so much!" I said excitedly. My mother gave me a kiss on the forehead before her and my father left.

"We'll figure everything out next weekend," she said.

I fell asleep that night smiling from ear to ear. I was thrilled.

The next Monday morning before school I stood in front of a closet full of clothes. So many choices and so many colors, yet, nothing to wear. Eventually I decided on a simple pair of jeans, a black t-shirt, and a pair of black flats. I went into the bathroom, ran a little gel through my damp locks, scrunched them up a bit, brushed on a dab of bronzer, applied some eyeliner and brushed my teeth. My mom dropped me off at school on her way to work. I ventured into the school building to meet my three best friends, Sophie, Taylor and Hailey, in the cafeteria, where we sat each morning before first period.

The four of us had been friends since kindergarten. We had slowly morphed into individuals as the years passed, but the trials and tribulations of teenagehood had brought us closer than ever.

Sophie is smart and quiet and never ceases to surprise me. She can completely hold her own and when it comes to being herself she is fearless.

Taylor and Sophie are slight opposites. Taylor wouldn't be considered too outgoing but is by no means shy. On the other hand she is still searching for herself. Her insecurities sometimes take over her mind as she struggles to accept who she is. She is beautiful.

Hailey and I are similar in the fact that we are completely outspoken. Hailey is very particular about things and she always does them exactly the same way. She is a compelling person, and most people are attracted to the atmosphere she creates.

As for myself, I must admit I'm a bit bossy. It's funny that all four of us are such different people and have different qualities but are best friends. We have separate lives but share a bond that completely connects us.

"Hey guys."

Sophie looked up from her science book and Taylor and Hailey from their cell phones.

"Mornin' sunshine!" Taylor yelped.

"Girls, stop what you're doing. I have some very important news," I said, my voice shaking. "Well," I paused.

"They said yes!"

"Oh my god! That's great!" Sophie said.

Hailey, who obviously didn't listen when I said, "Stop what your doing" looked up from her phone confused.

"What was that now?"

"Wait, I can't believe they agreed to let you go," Taylor said, ignoring Hailey's confusion.

My friends had known for a long time about my displeasure here and had been urging me to ask my parents for weeks.

"Wow. Now that they've said yes it's really sinking it," Sophie said. "You're really going.

"Six months without you," Taylor said.

"I'm so excited!" I said. "I didn't believe them when they said yes."

"Ugh," said Hailey, who had been opposed to the idea the entire time. "I mean, I understand if you need a change, but can't you get bangs or a new favorite color? Don't move to Antarctica!" she exclaimed.

I sighed. “Just be happy for me Hail. You know I love you.”

“What if you come back with all new friends and you don’t even like us anymore?”

“That will never happen,” I assured her.

After that day, the time just flew by. There were just two weeks left before my departure and as it grew closer to the day I knew that I was even more ready than I ever thought I could have been. I was going to live in another country, meet new people, and learn new customs. It is an entirely new culture. Since I found out that I was leaving, I had spoken on the phone with my uncle Jack who I’d be living with in Thurles. He seemed nice. He had such a strong accent, much stronger than my dad’s. I also spoke to the rest of the household, my aunt and two cousins. They were so friendly and acted like they couldn’t wait to meet me.

“Did you remember to bring your books home Sarah?” my mom said just as I walked in the door from school. “Finals are next week, so that means a lot of cramming until then.”

“Yes Mom, I remembered,” I said opening the fridge and pulling out the box of pizza from last night’s dinner. I took out a cold slice and began to devour it.

“Any second thoughts, sweetie?” she said.

I pulled my head out of the fridge in shock to see her sitting there smiling at me slyly.

“Hah. Yea right. I’m getting out of here,” I said, laughing, realizing she was being sarcastic.

I knew she wanted me to go, she was just going to miss me a lot. I would miss her too though. I had never been away from my parents for more than two weeks.

I left the kitchen still eating my pizza, went into the computer room and signed online. As soon as the welcome page

appeared for AOL Instant Messenger, I heard the sound of instant messages popping up onto the screen.

HotDevil33: I heard your parents are sending you away to Ireland. Is that true?

GoodieGumDrop69: Is it true your pregnant and have to go live with the nuns in Ireland?

CuseLuvr12: Good luck with rehab. It will be tough but you can do it.

Wow. I didn't even know those people and they thought they knew my deepest secret. In my high school, people will believe anything. All they need is a little bit of gossip to get them through the day. They feed off spreading rumors to make themselves feel better. News, whether it is true of false, apparently spreads fast. Someone had probably heard me talking about my trip that morning and formed an entirely ridiculous story. I deleted each box off the screen.

When I finished school on Friday I was prepared to have a weekend locked in my room studying. I had finals all next week before I left for Ireland and had only two days before my first exam. I went to the library after school to study. I walked home just as an orange sun was setting into the horizon and a cloudy white moon rose above the city. To my surprise, I arrived home to a dark and silent house. I walked in and dropped my backpack on the floor of the hallway. I flicked on the light switch and "Surprise!" My mom, my dad, Sophie, Taylor and Hailey jumped up from behind the couch.

"Oh my god! You guys scared the crap out of me!" I squealed back at them, my heart beating a mile a minute.

"We wanted to have a small, intimate, going away party!" Taylor said laughing.

The six of us sat down at the dining room table. My mom went into the kitchen and came out carrying a beautifully

decorated, homemade cake that had "We'll Miss You!" written on top of it.

"I slaved away all day making this cake, so it better be good!" my mom said.

After we had stuffed our faces with cake, my mom went back into the kitchen and re-appeared carrying three presents and an envelope.

"You guys didn't have to get me anything. Letting me go was the best present I could imagine," I said smiling.

Sophie, being the practical thinker that she is, bought me a debit card to use to write e-mail.

"It works just like a calling card," she explained. "You just go to the website on the back of the card and type in your code. If you don't write me every single memory I'll hurt you. I want to know every detail," she said, starting to cry. I gave her a big hug and promised her that I would write all the time.

Taylor bought me a picture frame with a picture of the four of us in it. On the top it said, "Friends Forever".

"That's so you won't forget us!" she said.

"How could I?" I grinned.

Hailey's present was a raincoat. For a while, we all sat there slightly puzzled when I pulled it out of the box and held it up. Everyone was silent until she finally broke the silence.

"Um, hello? You're going to the freaking rain capital of the world!"

We all went into a fit of laughter. Leave it to Hailey to lighten up a depressing mood.

Then, my mom handed me an envelope that said, "From Mom and Dad" on the front. I opened it up and inside was my ticket, one hundred euros, and a note. I read it aloud.

To Sarah,

Your father and I wish you the best of times in Ireland. It is such an amazing place and we know you will love it there. We wanted to do this for you because you deserve to see the world and experience a new culture. We will miss you so much but don't miss us too much because it will distract you from all the experiences.

Love, Mom and Dad

I was smiling from ear to ear and crying at the same time.

"Thank you so much. I am happy, sad, excited, and nervous all at the same time," I said wiping a tear from my smiling face.

"All right, all right, save the tears for the airport," my mom urged, holding back her own tears.

The girls slept over that night and we stayed up talking for hours. I agreed to write at least once a week, and I assured them, especially Hailey, that I would never forget them. After they fell asleep I lay there awake for some time. I thought about what my new school would be like and if I would make friends there. Thoughts swarmed my mind. I had no idea what to expect. But I was excited. I eventually fell asleep and drifted off to dreamland.

I saw a girl in a gorgeous dress, walking barefoot in a place surrounded by trees that I had never seen before. No one else was in sight. It was a serene place. Suddenly I spotted a boy watching her. He studied her as if she was a work of art, swiftly moving and hiding behind trees to catch her every angle. Their movements were in sync, yet they did not make eye contact. Their bodies were almost imaginary, moving so gracefully. The boy watched the girl intently as if afraid that if he took his eyes off her for one second she might disappear.

His features were just as remarkable as hers: deep blue eyes and short brown hair, and rosy cheeks, as if he had been running in the cold. She stopped moving and stood with her back to him. He slowly moved toward her. She sensed his presence. Their simple actions let me know that they in fact did know each other. There was a forbidden comfort between them. When he reached her he lightly touched her shoulder, barely skimming it with his fingertips. She brushed her cheek against his hand and closed her eyes. They couldn't look at each other. She wouldn't turn around and embrace him. Something was holding her back. They were both in pain and I could sense it. Suddenly they heard footsteps and quickly ran in opposite directions into the darkness.

When I woke up in the morning I was so confused. I didn't have a boyfriend or a "forbidden love" or even a crush. I opened my eyes and saw Sophie, Taylor and Hailey awake. I quickly forgot about the dream when I heard my stomach's loud growl.

"Anyone up for pancakes?" I asked.

"Definitely," the three of them responded at the same time, as they hopped out of their sleeping bags.

Chapter 2

"Do you have your ticket, passport, calling card, e-mailing card, money, and address book?"

"Mom. Just breathe. I've got everything."

"What about your toothbrush?"

"I'm pretty sure they have toothbrushes in Ireland," I said as we approached gate 23C. "Your uncle Eugene will be there when you get off the plane and he's going to take you to see your grandmother," my father said. "Then in a few days he'll take you to Jack's."

The attendant's voice came over the loud speaker. "This is the final call for rows fifteen through thirty-five."

"That's me," I said, looking at them. The three of us stood there, unsure of the next move. I dropped my bag and hugged them each goodbye, but my mother wouldn't let go. My dad pried her hands away from my waist and held onto them tight to reassure her that everything would be all right. I handed the attendant my ticket and turned around for one last look at them.

"I'll miss you," I said as I blew my mom one last kiss.

I walked down the tunnel and a strange feeling came over me. As I was stepping onto the plane I heard my mother yell, "Call as soon as you get in!"

I couldn't believe what I was doing. I would be away from my parents for six whole months. It was scary, and I liked the feeling.

Chapter 3

I closed my eyes as I wheeled my luggage out through the sliding doors of the Shannon airport. When I stepped outside, I stuck my nose way up into the air and inhaled the smell of my new home. It had that refreshing aroma of air just after the rain. I opened one eye, and then the other. I was in Ireland! I smiled as my surroundings were finally revealed to me.

"First time?"

I turned to see a man watching me. He was about fifty-five years old. He had gray hair and green eyes, and his face was rough looking; it must have been days since he last shaved. He was wearing a wool sweater and navy blue pants with brown shoes that seemed small and were worn down.

"Is it that obvious?" I said to him, laughing.

"I've never seen anyone enjoy the view of a dull sky and an airplane the way you just did," he said, laughing right back at me. I noticed he had a large, round gut that shook when he laughed.

A small car pulled up about ten yards from where I was standing with my luggage. A tall, burly man stepped out of the driver's seat. He began to approach me and said, "You must be Sarah. How are you keepin'?"

"Hi, nice to meet you," I said, sticking out my hand. His enormous hand swallowed it whole. "How'd you know it was me?" I asked.

"You've got American written all over you," he said smiling. "I'm Eugene, by the way."

"I'm assuming you're my uncle then."

"Right you are, Missus." He grabbed my two sixty-pound suitcases, one in each hand. I went to the door of the car and climbed in while he was still loading my belongings into the trunk. I turned my head forward, noticed a steering wheel directly in front of me, and began to laugh at my stupidity. He came to the window.

"Wrong side," he laughed.

Embarrassed, I opened the door and went to sit on the other side.

"I'll have to remember that," I said as I buckled my seatbelt. I waved goodbye to the man with the large belly as we drove away and he nodded and gave me a wink. We drove for a couple miles in silence. As the kilometers passed, it seemed like we were going farther and farther into the country. There were endless acres of land covered with the greenest grass my eyes had ever seen. The rolling hills were like quilts that covered the countryside. As we drove around bends and over hills, I was beginning to get a slight case of carsickness. Eugene turned to me and said, "Jesus! Your face is nearly the color of the grass out there. Are you sick, child?"

I held in my laughter so as not to offend him. His accent was much stronger than my father's and I was still getting used to it. We came to a stop after a couple of minutes and I looked ahead to see what the hold up was.

"Just a little traffic jam, that's all. It's common down around here."

I was confused because I hadn't recalled seeing many other cars. As we inched along we came closer to the "traffic jam," which was mooooooooooing. I counted thirteen cows walking down the road being led by a boy around my age. I stared at him in amazement as we passed by and he glanced at me and tipped his hat. I laughed hysterically inside and couldn't wait

to tell Sophie about my first Irish traffic jam. After we drove by, Eugene finally broke the silence.

"So, how was the flight over? Did you sleep at all?"

"No, I couldn't sleep, I was too excited."

"I bet you're going to love it here. You'll be staying with your uncle Jack, won't you?"

"I talked to him on the phone a couple times, and he said he has the situation with my school already figured out."

"I'll take you down to meet Biddy before I take you over to the park, right?"

I didn't know what he was talking about but I agreed anyways. I could barely understand him, he was talking so fast.

We drove through a few towns and through more of the countryside. The ride must have taken about an hour and a half, but the time passed by quickly. Eugene answered all my questions about the town and the family until I was fully acquainted with his Ireland. He listed everyone's name through the first cousins. I learned I have seven uncles, an aunt, and thirty some cousins.

"The Irish are the friendliest people in the world," Eugene declared.

He also snuck in a small history lesson on the way as we passed multiple castles.

When we arrived in Thurles, the town where the family lives, he showed me around, which didn't take long at all. He pointed out a few of the thirty-two pubs in Thurles, including one that the family owned years ago. Finally, we ended up at a house with an imposing gate. We strolled up the driveway, where all was quiet and still. It was a large stone house with an enormous yard. The yard was home to six stables for horses and a riding arena.

"My daughter, Laura Ellen, rides, and yours aunt Mary gives lessons as well," he said. "I myself love horses. I breed them; some to use and ride, some to sell."

I followed Eugene in through the back door, into the kitchen, to a silent almost deadly quiet house. A woman was sitting at the table looking out the window. Her figure was so peaceful as she sat sipping a cup of tea and occasionally referring back to the newspaper in front of her. She had thin gray hair, which was tied up in a small bun, and pale soft skin. She wore thick glasses, a worn out nightgown, and slippers. She turned and saw me watching her. I smiled, but she did not immediately return the gesture.

"Hello Sarah, home from America, are we?" she said, almost ardently.

"This is Biddy, your granny and my mother," Eugene said.

"Come sit down, do you want a cup of tea? How was the flight? Jesus, you must be wrecked, pet. Do you want to go to sleep?"

I was slightly confused by all the questions being thrown at me, but I realized that I was actually kind of tired.

"Eugene, bring her upstairs and let her sleep, will ya?" she said. "You can come down after you get some rest and have you're dinner later, and then we can have a nice chat when you're all rested."

"Okay, I guess," I said. I followed Eugene down a corridor and upstairs to a bedroom. He left me and said he would see me in a few hours and that I should catch up on my sleep. As soon as my head hit the pillow I was asleep; I didn't even have time to soak in the reality of being in this strange and beautiful land.

Chapter 4

I woke to a salty and sweet aroma that had drifted up the stairs and into the room, arousing my senses, convincing me to get out of bed and head downstairs where I heard voices in the kitchen. I was nervous to get out of bed and face those noises, but decided that I had to make the best of the situation, not to mention, I was starving. As I walked down the stairs, I noticed photographs that were hanging on the wall. There were a few of beautiful horses running wild, boys playing a sport that I didn't even recognize, and one of a couple standing in front of a house. I recognized the woman as a much younger Biddy. I continued walking downstairs and came upon a little boy and girl staring directly at me. The boy was about five years old. He had the largest blue eyes I had ever seen and his hands and face were filthy, almost stained as if he had never washed them. The girl, about two years old, also had a stained face, only not with dirt. Her "marking" appeared to be ketchup. They looked shyly upward at me from the bottom of the stairs, but said nothing. Nonetheless, I said hello.

I continued down the hall and opened the door to the kitchen. A cloud of smoke formed a halo around my head. I turned to see four men sitting around the table. One was Eugene, and another, the boy from the picture who was now grown into a man. He was tall with light brown hair cut very short on his head. He was obviously a couple years older than me, for his face was rough with stubble that in a few days would be a full grown beard. He looked almost the same as in the picture, which must have been at least ten years ago, only his features were much more mature and bold. Biddy was sitting on a tall stool in front of the stove, and a woman who looked vaguely familiar was standing in front of the sink staring out the big window that looked into the yard. She turned, saw me and smiled.

"Well Sarah! How are ya?" she came towards me and gave me a hug. "I'm your Aunty Mary."

"Hi, it's nice to meet you," I said, rubbing my eyes, which were irritated by the thick white smoke that filled the room.

"Did you meet Bill and Eimear in the hall there? Those are two of my children," she said.

"Wait, is this John's young one?" said one of the men at the table. He was much shorter than Eugene and was quite stocky. He was smoking a cigarette and drinking a cup of tea. The other man didn't say much. He was average height and had very dark brown hair. He had a cap on his head that left a dark shadow across his eyes.

"This is Sarah. Sarah, this is Pat, Kevin, Paul, and you already know Eugene," Mary said, pointing them out one by one. "Now, Sarah, just a little warning for you, you're related to a lot of people around here, so you'll just have to do your best to remember them all. Pat, Kevin, and Eugene are your father's brothers and Paul is your cousin and my son.

"Well, how ya keepin'?" Paul and Kevin said at the same time.

"Nice to meet you too," I said, unsure if that was the correct answer to their question.

I went over to the stove and stood next to Biddy and watched her carefully as she peeled the potatoes for dinner. When she noticed me watching her so intently, she reached into the drawer pulled out another peeler and handed it to me. I picked up a potato and watched her as I peeled to make sure I did it the right way. Her strokes were smooth but quick and I had to go much slower. While she sat there in silence, with me standing next to her peeling potatoes, I remembered a poem by Seamus Heaney that my father had once recited to me:

When all the others were away at Mass
I was all hers as we peeled potatoes.
They broke the silence, let fall one by one
Like solders weeping off the soldering iron:
Cold comforts set between us, things to share
Gleaming in a bucket of clean water.
And again let fall. Let pleasant splashes
From each other's work would bring us to our senses.

I smiled to think that my father probably liked the poem because he had spent plenty of afternoons peeling potatoes with his mother. Now I was peeling potatoes with her, too.

Eugene looked up from the table and asked me if I was going to stay here for a few days before I went to live with my uncle Jack.

"Of course she'll stay," Biddy said.

"Right, so, I'll bring your bags up to the room for you later," Eugene said. As soon as dinner was ready, Biddy fed Eugene, Pat, Kevin, and Paul. The three of them ate their food at the speed of light and left to get back to work. The kitchen seemed less chaotic with just Biddy, Mary, and I, and I was able to sit down at the table and talk with them.

"I'm really happy to be here," I told them.

"We're delighted to have you," Mary said. "I can't believe I haven't even seen my brother since you were only a baby. It's like a little bit of John is here as well."

"You think I'm similar to him?"

"I don't know, I'll have to see you mad in order to tell," she said, laughing.

After I devoured my dinner we had a cup of tea and apple tart. I told them all about our lives in Syracuse and about Mom and Dad. I noticed something about Mary rather quickly. She is one of those people who, when she has something to say, she compels everyone to listen. She spoke the same as Biddy, very gracefully, and full of wisdom. They both sounded as though they had so much knowledge when they spoke, and they were very convincing about it. When Mary talked about her life, I was truly interested in hearing what she had to say. They then went on to tell me about my father's horrible temper as a child, and I guaranteed them that it had followed him into adulthood.

"His elder brothers were always giving him their clothes when they got too small," Mary began.

"And boy, did he hate getting them old clothes," Biddy said. "Anyways, Connor gave him a gorgeous jacket one winter and your father was so mad whenever he had to wear it. When he came home from school one day, I asked him where the jacket had gone and he said, very boldly and tough, 'I threw it in the river'," she laughed. "Your grandfather was so mad; I'd say Matt's bum is still black and blue!"

Mary was sitting across from the table laughing hysterically. I too was in a fit of laughter. I couldn't imagine my dad doing that.

After a while, Biddy went off to take her afternoon rest and Mary told me she had to go downtown to run an errand. I went into the sitting room, or living room, as we would call it, and sat down. About five minutes into my channel surfing, Paul and two other boys strode up the driveway. They came into the sitting room and grabbed the remote from me.

"Hey look lads, it's the yank," said one of the boys. He was tall with blond hair and bright blue eyes. He was tossing a soccer ball up in the air.

"Actually my name's Sarah. I'm John's daughter."

"Actually, I'm John's daughter," the boy said, faking an American accent and mocking me.

"Are we related?" I asked in a somewhat snotty tone.

"Unfortunately, yes," said the other boy.

Put off by their rudeness, I didn't respond. Paul, the oldest, noticed my silence and sudden passive attitude.

"Aw, we're just messin' with ya," Paul said. "That's James and Eoghan. They're your cousins as well."

I took from this conversation that James and Eoghan were slightly less mature than Paul, I was pretty sure Paul was the oldest. Paul had the remote now and flicked to some sports game. I noticed that it was the same game Paul was playing in the pictures that I had noticed on my way downstairs. I asked him what it was. He looked shocked when I asked him, but thankfully didn't ridicule me.

"That's called Rugby. Have you never heard of it?"

"Never," I said.

"It's a great game. We'll have to teach you sometime," Paul said. James and Eoghan both snickered. I ignored their contempt for my ignorance.

"That would be cool," I said.

We sat silently for a minute as we all concentrated on the game.

"So how old are you anyways?" Eoghan said, trying to make normal conversation.

"I'm fifteen. How old are you?"

"I'm fourteen, James is seventeen, and Paul is twenty."

"Now, I know we're all related but give me a little overview."

"Right, James and I are Pat's kids. Paul is Mary's."

"Oh, okay gotcha," I replied, trying to match the names with the faces of the men I had met earlier. It was going to take me a while to remember everyone. Back home I saw my mom's side of the family a couple of times a year, but in Ireland, I was going to see my family every day. I was already beginning to love how different it was living with my Irish family, including the disarray and atmosphere of the house.

We watched the rest of the game, and after an hour or so Mary came back. She asked Paul to do something for her that I didn't quite understand. James and Eoghan were going as well.

"You goin' for the spin?" Mary asked me.

"Um, sure, I guess." I followed Paul, James, and Eoghan outside and we climbed into a big red work van. We drove through the town and down through country roads, sitting silently in the car as the radio played *The Zephyr Song* by the Red Hot Chili Peppers. We drove through a field down a little dirt road and stopped just outside a gate connected to a fenced-in field. Paul opened the trunk of the van, which was filled with hay. He ordered James, Eoghan, and I to each grab a barrel and follow him. When I got to the gate, four beautiful horses were grazing in the field straight ahead of me. As soon as they noticed we had hay, they began to approach us. I had ridden a horse once or twice but always with someone holding onto a lead. I loved their character, the way they moved, and their body language toward other horses and toward people. I found them to be fascinating creatures. Obviously, the boys didn't think so because as soon as they had released the hay from the twine, we left. I, on the other hand, could have stayed

and watched for hours. Thankfully, the car ride home was not in silence. I asked them about school and about people their age. I was curious as to what everyone did for fun, and I was curious to hear what they had to say about the school I would be attending.

"We go to pubs and nightclubs on the weekends," James said. "Or house parties."

"We just hang out," Eoghan said.

When we arrived back at Biddy's, there were people out in the arena. I saw Mary and Eimear standing in the middle while someone rode a horse around. James and Eoghan said they were going home and Paul had to go back down to work. I walked down into the arena to talk to Mary and Eimear.

"What's going on?" I asked.

"Nothing. That's Nora up there on the horse. She's your cousin as well," Mary said, never taking her eyes off the girl or the horse.

"That's Twiggy, Nora's pony," Eimear said pointing to the horse.

After Nora rode around a couple more laps of the arena and jumped a couple poles, she trotted over to where Mary, Eimear, and I were standing.

"Hey, who are you?" she said, still atop the horse.

"I'm Sarah, John's daughter from America."

"Oh, ya! I didn't know when you were coming over. Did daddy pick you up from the airport this morning?"

"Eugene picked me up this morning," I replied, unsure of who her father was in this large and complicated family.

"Ya, that's Daddy!" she said as she hopped off her horse. The four of us walked up from the arena back into the yard. Nora

took Twiggy's saddle and bridles off and put her into a stable. Then she went into some sort of shed and took off her helmet and back protector. She linked her arm inside of mine and we started walking. It wasn't until she took off her gear that I could actually see her face. She was very pretty with hazel eyes and shoulder length light brown hair. She had a very young looking face and I didn't think she was much older than thirteen. She was also extremely tall and skinny. I could see that Eugene was her father because he was also very tall. She had on a sweatshirt of some sort, tight little tan riding pants, and riding boots.

"Have you been down the shop yet?" she said happily.

"Um, what shop?" I responded, looking totally clueless.

"Our shop! It's across the street. How'd you miss it? Daddy owns it!"

It was a small yellow building with royal blue accents that said "Ryan's" at the top. We went inside and Nora said hello to the girl working at the cash register. It was like an American supermarket, just much smaller.

"There's a restaurant in the back that just opened as well!" she said. "I can't believe I'm only meeting you now and we're first cousins! How old are you anyway?" She kept shooting questions at me as she went behind the counter and grabbed a handful of gummy candies.

"I know. It's really weird coming here having never met any of my family. I'm fifteen. How about you?"

"I'm thirteen," she said; just as I had suspected.

"Are you hungry? Do you want some sweets or crisps?"

"I actually don't have any Euro yet. I have to exchange it first," I told her. "And what are crisps?"

"Oh, um, like American chips! Sorry, I forgot! It's fine, grab whatever you want."

"Okay. Do you suggest anything?"

"Here, have a Cadbury's Dairy Milk. I bet you don't have chocolate this delicious in the States."

I ripped open the wrapper and took a bite. It was amazing. The sweet, milky mixture melted in my mouth. "Wow! That is by far the best chocolate I have ever tasted."

She laughed and grabbed my hand, pulling me down the aisles. At the back of the store there was a butcher and a hot food counter. She pulled me inside an office. Eugene, Paul, and Pat were all inside. I came to the conclusion that Paul and Pat also worked at the shop.

"Well Sarah, how are you getting on?"

"Fine. I just tasted the best chocolate in the world."

"Daddy, is the door unlocked? Sarah and I are going up to the house."

"I think it's locked actually, but your mother's home."

"Alright, see you later." Before we left the shop, we each grabbed a handful of sweets. We walked along, past rows of houses. Nora pointed out a white house with a sign that said "Melrose" out front.

"That's where Pat and his family live," she said. We arrived at Nora's house. It was stone and painted a very light peach color. There was a small garden in the front and a big fence that enclosed the backyard. The door was unlocked and I followed Nora inside. It was filled with photographs of Nora and other people I had never seen before and pictures that someone had painted. There was a giant statue of a lion and a giraffe and baskets filled with various noise makers from Africa.

"Mom and Dad love Africa, if you couldn't tell. Also, Mom's very crafty. She loves to paint, sew, bead, you name it, and she does it. See, here I am at the beach and me riding Twiggy, but she painted those ages ago." The house was nicer than Biddy's. The floors were clean, the walls intact, and the layer of dust much thinner. I heard a voice upstairs calling Nora's name.

"Nora, is that you?"

"Hi Mom! I'm home! I brought Sarah over. She just came in this morning," Nora called back.

"Bring her upstairs so I can meet her!" We walked upstairs to a small loft. It was filled with boxes of fabrics, beads, yarns, paints, and brushes. A woman with short wavy brown hair looked up from the sewing machine where she was working.

"Hi Sarah! It's so nice to finally meet you. How was the flight over dear?"

"Nice to meet you too. Oh it was fine, a couple of crying babies, a little turbulence, the usual, I suppose." I turned my head to get a better view of the room. There was a computer sitting on a desk in the corner. I wanted to ask to use it but I wasn't comfortable doing that yet. It would be a little while before I was fully acquainted with everyone and used to being here all the time.

Nora dragged me back downstairs to watch a movie. She put a movie in and sat down on the couch. The screen changed from black and some music began to play.

"I love this movie!" I exclaimed as I realized that it was *Ten Things I Hate about You*.

"Yea, me too!"

After the movie was over, I realized that I'd lost all perception of the time. I asked Nora, who then pointed in the direction of

a clock. It was six o'clock in the evening, which meant it was one o'clock in the afternoon in my head. Nora asked me if I wanted to sleep over and said that we could rent another movie or something. We walked back down to Biddy's so I could get pajamas and a toothbrush and make sure it was all right with Mary if I stayed with Nora. Mary said of course it was all right. Biddy was sitting in a chair in the sitting room watching the news. I walked in to let her know that I was sleeping down at Nora's house. She asked me if I would like to help her cook the dinner tomorrow and said we could make another apple tart together.

"I would love to help you tomorrow."

"I'm cooking a chicken because it's Sunday," she said. "But of course we will have potatoes with it, and you, my dear, need much more practice," she said with a slight smile on her face. I smiled back at her and quietly left the room.

Nora and I took a shortcut back to her house by going through James and Eoghan's backyard. We watched another movie and talked for a while. She was a nice girl and I was looking forward to getting to know her, but I hoped to meet some girls my own age that I could relate to much better. She fell asleep much earlier than I did and I was restless in this strange place I had never been before. I snuck out of my sleeping bag on the floor and quietly tiptoed down the hallway upstairs to in front of the computer.

As soon as the computer had booted up, I clicked on the Internet link and checked my mail. It had only been a day since I checked it and I didn't have any unread messages. I saw that there was an icon for AOL Instant Messenger on the desktop so I clicked on it and signed online. I instantly received three messages from my girls! At first I was confused

because it was 12:30 a.m. but I realized that back home, it was only 7:30 p.m.

ꟾ ꟾ

HaileysComet32: Oh my god! Oh my god! How is it??? How was the flight??? How are you??? What's your family like? I'm so happy to talk to you!!

SarBear15: Hey Hailey! It's beautiful here! The flight was okay, a little scary. It's so different here.

Polarbear99: Hey!!! How's Ireland?!?!?!

SarBear15: Oh my god Sophie! You would love it here! I love it here already. It's beautiful!

TayTay101: Hey World Traveler! How's Ireland!!! Seen any hotties yet?? We miss you!

SarBear15: Hey Tay! It's awesome! Nope, no hotties yet, but I'll keep you posted.

Then, I decided I would send each of them the same messages to make it easier. Anyway, they all had the same questions.

SarBear15: It's so green here. I love it. There are animals everywhere: Sheep, cows and horses! I met my grandmother for the first time today since I was like two months old. I met a bunch of my uncles, my aunt, and a couple of cousins. It's hard to remember everyone's names and whose kids they are. Anyway I'm going to live with my grandmother for a couple of nights before I go to live with my uncle Jack for the rest of

the time. I'm really hoping to start riding horses while I'm here! I haven't seen any cute boys yet but I know there are some around here somewhere! I really like my cousin Nora. She's thirteen and she's very nice. As soon as I start taking pictures I'll send them over. I haven't needed my raincoat yet and I look at pictures of you every day! Now that I've filled you in I have to go. I miss you loads and I'll talk to you soon! Love you!

HaileysComet32: Love you and miss you too! Have fun!

❧ ☙

Polarbear99: Love you so much! Make memories! Be safe!

❧ ☙

TayTay101: Be good! Have fun! Miss you bunches!

❧ ☙

I turned of the computer and tiptoed back downstairs and into Nora's room. Somehow I was satisfied having talked to my friends and was able to fall asleep as soon as I was back in my sleeping bag on the floor.

Chapter 5

Around eleven o'clock Sunday morning Eugene brought me over to Jack's house, where I would be staying for the duration of my stay.

"Thanks for everything Eugene," I said when we got into the van.

"Anything you need, you just give me a call," he said. I smiled at his generosity.

"And you know you are welcome at my house or Biddy's whenever you want."

"Thanks. I may take you up on that," I said.

When we arrived at Jack's he said a quick hello and unloaded my things from the van. I watched him drive away, and then turned around to where my uncle Jack, aunt Una, and my cousins Grainne and Aisling were standing. They helped me carry my things inside their small townhouse in Childers Park, about a mile from Biddy's house. In the front of the house there was a small rose garden, and at the back there was a shed filled with bikes, tools, a clothes drier, and other various pieces of junk, and a clothesline. I wondered where they kept their car.

"You must have a small car that fits back here," I exclaimed jokingly.

"We don't have one," Jack said.

"You're not in a America anymore darlin'!" Una said laughing. I grew slightly embarrassed, but recovered quickly.

"Mum and Daddy ride their bikes to work," Aisling said.

"And Aisling and I take the train back and forth from school," Grainne added.

I followed Aisling, Grainne, Jack, and Una up the narrow staircase as they gave me the grand tour of their home. We went into a small bedroom that was painted pink and purple. There was a small television, a double bed, a single bed, two dressers, and a nightstand, plus it had a closet. I scanned the room. The double bed was covered with stuffed animals, and the wall just behind it was lined with pictures. I recognized a few people; Paul, Jack, Una, Mary, Biddy. The top of one dresser was covered with bottles of perfume, lotion, sunless tanning products, hair products, and hairbrushes. The other dresser had only a CD player and a lamp on it. There was an enormous window that looked out into the back yard and over past many other houses. The windowsill was covered with trophies and medals, but I was too far away from them and could hardly read the inscriptions. The room was extremely cluttered and I wondered where all of my things would go. I assumed that the three of us would be sharing it. Eek. I guess it could work.

"Sorry it's so small, but Grainne and I are barely here during the week so it won't be cramped all the time," Aisling said.

"Oh, no, it's great. It's, um, very cozy," I said, slightly sarcastically. I was pretty certain that it was going to be anything but great, as I was used to having a room larger than this all to myself back home.

After the introductions and the millions of questions, Jack and Una left the room. Aisling and Grainne sat on the double bed while I sat on the single. They were both in college, but returned home on the weekends. Their sister, Niamh, attended

college in New Jersey to play basketball. My father once told me that I resembled Niamh. She was the eldest of the three girls. Aisling was the middle child. Her shoulder length hair was dyed dark brown, which complemented her dark eyes. Grainne was the youngest. Her hair was longer than Aisling's, and it too was dyed dark brown, but in certain light had a slight red tint. Grainne was much taller than Aisling, and her body was long and lean. Like Niamh, Grainne was a basketball player. Niamh, I could tell from the pictures on the wall, wasn't a girly type and she was very naturally pretty. I soon came to realize that the pink walls and stuffed animals were Aisling's decorating ideas; she was the opposite of Niamh. I hoped that Aisling and Grainne and I would become close. After all, we were sharing a room the size of a prison cell for six months.

They asked me questions about my life at home. Did I have a boyfriend? What my school was like? What did I like to do for fun? Eventually, after I stopped answering, I started asking. They gave me the low down on the school and the town. Grainne had generously cleared out a few drawers for me to use, so I was able to begin unpacking. I decided to put my shirts in the dresser, my pants in the closet and my shoes under the bed. Everything else I left in my suitcase, which I also shoved under the bed. After a while the three of us wandered back downstairs and into the kitchen, where Una had just boiled a pot of tea.

"Well Sarah. Did you unpack? Is everything okay? Are you all right pet? Anything you ever need, just ask me."

"Thanks Una," I said responding to her multiple questions all at once.

"Would you like a cup of tea? Do you want anything to eat? How about a chicken fillet or some soup? I can't believe I have nothing for you. I'll go to the shop. What would you like?" she said, overwhelming me.

"It's okay I'm not hungry. I'll have a cup of tea though." I sat and talked to Una for about twenty minutes. After I finished my tea I went upstairs and sat on the single bed while Aisling and Grainne shuffled about the room, getting ready to go out for the night. I finally went to sleep after laying out my uniform for the morning. Around three a.m. the two girls stumbled upstairs and into the room. I heard them as they did their best to move around in the dark room but I kept my eyes closed and pretended I was asleep.

It was my first day at my new school, The Presentation, and I was already late. I woke with plenty of time to shower, get dressed, and eat breakfast, but somehow the walk through town and down to the school took much longer than I had expected. I had started the morning feeling prepared and ready, but now, for some reason, I was nervous. I walked through the silent parking lot, which was filled with deserted cars, up to the front door of the school. I noticed pairs of eyes peeking out at me from the windows of a classroom on the first floor. They knew I was an outsider. They could smell my fear all the way underneath my burgundy pleated skirt and burgundy wool jumper. I looked down to make sure each piece of my uniform was intact. My burgundy socks were pulled up to my knees, my striped tie was straight, and my cream button down shirt was neatly pressed. I walked through the door and stood in the main hallway, hoping that a principal would come by and ask me if I was lost. A woman with blond

hair popped out of an office to the right of me and said, "You must be Sarah. We've been waiting for you."

Another woman with blond hair rounded the corner and smiled widely at me. "Hello Sarah. I'm Miss Dwyer, the principal of the school."

She was friendly looking and slightly eased my nervousness. Miss Dwyer asked me to follow her. We walked through the school until we reached a door, which I suspected was my classroom. Miss Dwyer entered first and I followed. The students in the classroom immediately stood for her entry. I was shocked by the respect she received from the students because in my school, you never stood for a teacher. I avoided eye contact with the other girls, but took a quick glance around the room. It was a fairly big room with a dry erase board, a podium at the front, and small lockers in the back. On two of the walls crosses were hung along with a small statue of Mary. The room was cold and uninviting. The walls were badly painted and chipping, and had no colorful posters or motivational sayings on them as most American classrooms have. I estimated about twenty-five girls sitting before me, smiling through their teeth and staring me up and down, trying to figure out who exactly I was. As soon as Miss Dwyer finished my introduction she quietly left the room. The teacher sitting on a stool behind the podium introduced herself as Miss Darcy and directed me to an open seat in the third row. She suggested that we all get somewhat acquainted before we started the lesson. The girl in front of me turned around to introduce herself. She was a thick girl with shoulder length dark brown hair and enormous dark eyes. She instantly started babbling on to me.

"Oh my god. You're Sarah! From America! How many movie stars do you know? Have you been to New York City? Do you

walk down the street and see famous people everywhere? Oh yea, I almost forgot I'm Maebh!" She was practically close enough to kiss me. Her aggressive introduction frightened me, but I knew she meant well.

"Hi," I said. "No, movie stars aren't everywhere," I said laughing.

A girl with curly hair and glasses sat at the front of the classroom and abruptly shouted out, "Are you like in High School? Are you a cheerleader and you go out with the quarterback?" I laughed hard, but quickly stopped so I would avoid offending her. I didn't want to make any enemies on the first day of school.

"High school is really only like that in movies. I'm far from a cheerleader and I don't hang out with football players." She turned back to the front of the class with the most disappointed facial expression.

"That's Colleen," said a girl to my right. She was leaning up against the windows. She was tall and stringy and had long brown hair and brown eyes. Her features were simple but put together in an appealing way. She sat next to five of her friends who were talking and every now and then taking a quick glance at me.

"Hi, I'm Sarah. I noticed the six of you staring at me as I was walking in this morning."

"Yea, sorry, we thought it was you but we weren't sure. I'm Kate, and this is Sinead, Deirdre, Amy, Kiara, and Mairead."

"Hey guys!" I responded happily. We talked for a couple minutes and I became more familiar with them and their school. They asked me where I was from and why I had decided to come here for six months. They begged me to tell

them about America and were so interested to hear about the differences between our countries.

I was really looking forward to making friends with all the girls. I walked around and continued to introduce myself to everyone.

After first period was over we had Math, then Geography. The classes went by extremely slow and I found them all to be boring and dull. Then we had a break to get a snack and relax before our next three classes. There was a place to get rolls and freshly baked bread with butter and jam or chocolate doughnuts, and two little shops to buy sweets, drinks, and crisps (as I now called them) right inside the school. I bought a plain doughnut with creamy chocolate filling and went back to sit in the classroom. It was pretty much empty except for a few girls because most were off buying snacks or talking with friends from other classes. Thankfully, Deirdre and Sinead walked in, also eating doughnuts, and sat down in two of the chairs next to me.

"So what in the world ever made you want to come here? It's so boring in Thurles," Deirdre said as she scooped the jam out of her doughnut with her index finger and licked it off.

"Well, let's see. I guess for starters I was just really restless at home. Like if you went to live in my town for six months I would probably think you were crazy too."

"I guess that makes sense," Sinead said. "I'll be back. I want to buy another doughnut."

"Also, I have so much family here that I have never met because we never come over to visit," I added.

"You should come more often then!" she said.

"I wish it was that easy."

The bell rang, signaling the end of our break, and Deirdre went back over to her seat. "We'll talk more at lunch," she said. All of the other girls filed inside the classroom and sat down in their seats, quickly finishing the last crumbs of their snacks before class began.

We now had computer with the only male teacher in the entire school, Mr. Malloy. We called him Sir, just as we called the entire female staff Miss. Respect for teachers at the Presentation was much different from my school in Syracuse. Mr. Malloy was a strange man with enormous eyes that bugged right out of his head. I guessed he was about forty-five years old and aging was definitely not on his side. When I introduced myself, I stuck out my hand, in which he shook strongly with his chubby, dry hand. He reeked of cigarette smoke. In addition to his strange looks, he appeared to have a great deal of trouble controlling a class of twenty-five girls. I felt bad for him in a way because he was so helpless.

After computer, I was forced to make a choice between French or German, neither of which I spoke. The girls were in their fourth year of their language and either way, I would be lost in France or Germany. Colleen convinced me to go to German with her because she claimed they didn't do much of anything in class. Basically, I just sat and listened and misunderstood. Occasionally, the teacher, Miss Kelley would try to teach me a word or two but nothing stuck. After German we had gym class. It was different at my co-ed school, where the sexes would separate into locker rooms to change. Here, all of us girls changed clothes right in the classroom. We ran a few laps around the "gym", which was also the cafeteria and the theater, and then played badminton for a while.

Finally, it was lunchtime. I watched as Kate made her way over to the table, her long legs gracefully moving toward the table. I sat silently for a couple of minutes observing them. Deirdre was so funny. She had a lot to say.

"Deirdre, do you mind moving down so I can sit next to Kiara," asked Mairead.

"Sure, no problem," Deirdre responded, acting like the easy going person I had already noticed her to be. She had long blond hair and extremely pale skin.

Sinead and Amy were very similar to one another. They were both kind of shy at first, but they eventually opened up. They both had shoulder-length brown hair and lots of freckles. Mairead was definitely shy and seemed uncomfortable around me because she didn't know me. I saw her looking at me. When we would make eye contact she would smile and turn away quickly. I could tell she was talkative because I saw her being open and loud with the other girls. I guessed it would just take time. She was very simple and elegant. She had shoulder length strawberry blond hair and gorgeous skin. It looked like she had blush on all the time but it was a completely natural glow to her skin. Finally, I tried to figure out Kiara. She and I had hit it off completely. She had thick black hair and hazel eyes. She was really cool to talk to and we had a lot in common. I was zoning out and staring at them all when Deirdre snapped me out of it.

"Hello, earth to Sarah," she said snapping her fingers in front of my face.

"Oh sorry! I was daydreaming." They were all halfway into their lunches by now, looking at me oddly.

Anyone I should steer clear of?" I asked.

"No, I would say you can handle everybody," Kiara said.

I had ordered a ham sandwich at break time that arrived for lunch. I gobbled it down fast because I was so hungry. I had brought a yogurt and an apple from home and then decided to buy a bag of crisps from the shop.

"So what do you like about Thurles so far?" Kate asked.

"Um, I like my family a lot, but probably my favorite thing is the chocolate! I love it! I can't get enough of it! I swear I will gain twenty pounds before I go home!" They all laughed at me.

"My father told me the chocolate in America is rotten. Ye don't even have Cadbury Chocolate," Kiara said. All the girls at the table gasped.

"I don't know what I would do without Cadbury," Sinead exclaimed stuffing a piece of a bar of chocolate in her mouth at that very moment.

As we continued with our lunches I asked them about what they did on the weekends.

"Some weekends we'll go out to this nightclub called the Ragg," Kate said. "It's class."

"Class?" I asked.

"Yea, class. Like it's fun. A good laugh like," she explained.

"Oh, okay. Gotcha."

"You'll definitely have to come sometime with us!" Amy said excitedly.

"All right cool! Ya know what I've noticed? I haven't seen any cute boys around here since I came over. Somcone please tell me they're around," I said laughing.

"Oh yea, there's plenty of good-looking lads," Kiara said smiling. "You should hang around town with us after school. Most days we don't go home until six o'clock or so."

"Okay, sure," I said just as the bell rang ending lunch. We rose from our seats and cleared the table off. Science and English were the last two classes of the day. I followed the girls up to the third floor of the school and into the biology lab. We sat in the back of the classroom while the teacher gave a lecture and we took notes. The teacher, Miss McGraw, was a very pretty, young woman. I was shocked when she entered the class because she was so young and pretty, quite different from all the other teachers who were mostly old and tired, not to mention quite stiff. For English, we were split up into two different classes with two different teachers. My teacher, Miss Calloway, was a thin woman who was slightly hunched over and wore glasses. She had short red hair which she carefully tucked behind her ears. She wore a long skirt and a cardigan, neither of which complimented her body type. She looked and dressed like an English teacher, or a librarian even, pardon my stereotyping. She walked into class, stood behind the podium, and began to explain the lesson. Colleen, who was sitting next to me, was fiddling with her pen as Miss Calloway spoke.

"Stop clicking pens! Stop clicking pens! That's the one thing I ask! Just stop clicking pens!" she exclaimed.

Colleen and I looked at each other in shock, covered our mouths and started to laugh hysterically. Miss Calloway turned around and gave a cold and harsh look, which we inferred as a demand to keep quiet. We passed notes all

through class because Miss Calloway kept her back to us while she scribbled nonsense on the board. When the bell to end the day finally rang, the other class rejoined us in the room and we gathered our things to go home. Kiara, Kate, Deirdre, Amy and I were going to walk around the town for a while, but Sinead and Mairead had field hockey practice. We walked out of the school, past a couple of pubs and a Chinese restaurant, over the bridge, and right into the heart of town. Students from all the different schools around were scattered throughout, walking to catch a bus home, window-shopping, eating, or standing around talking. I must have counted at least four other uniforms in addition to ours. The town had a wide variety of stores. There were two different grocery stores, a bunch of shops for women's and men's clothing, a handful of shops where you could buy sweets, magazines, and various other small things, two athletic shops, a post office, a hotel, a fast food place called Supermax, a book shop, a shop that sold school supplies, a couple of shoe stores, a movie shop, a couple of pharmacies, three banks, and more pubs than I could count on two hands and two feet. We weaved in and out of shops, looking at the latest fashions. We walked up the square towards where there were many groups deep in conversation.

"See look Sarah, there are loads of cute lads!" Kiara said as she scoped around for one to point out. "See there's one. He's lovely looking. I think I've seen him out at the Ragg a few times."

"Kiara, you can only see the back of his head. How do you know he's nice looking?" I said, laughing at her silliness.

"Well he has nice hair and a nice butt anyways," she said smiling at me.

"I think I've met him before," Kate said.

"Met him?" I asked.

"Yea, like kissed him. Pulled him," she explained. "What do you call it in America?"

"Hooked up," I said. "I need to start reviewing your Irish lingo. I'm beginning to get very confused," I said laughing some more.

"He just turned around, and he is cute. Just as I expected!" Kiara said. A group of people was in front of me blocking my vision from the so-called "cute boy," and as soon as they moved, I had a good view of him.

"Ew! That's my cousin! I can't believe we were staring at his butt!" I screamed.

"Oh! Sorry! What's his name?" she asked.

"James," I said loudly. Apparently I said it much louder than I thought because I caught his attention. He gave me a little nod and I waved. He was standing with a group of guys who were all actually quite good looking. I started zoning out again as this one boy in particular caught my eye. Deirdre grabbed my arm as we started walking across the street but I couldn't stop staring. I looked straight into his gorgeous blue eyes but it seemed as though it wasn't my first time. It was like I had seen him before somewhere. He looked straight at me with his short, messy, brown hair and rosy cheeks. Deirdre snapped her fingers in front of my face and I snapped out of my haze. I started walking across the street with her and turned around to catch another glimpse of the boy, but he was gone. I looked in every direction for the mystery boy's face, but it was too crowded and everywhere I turned, there was a brown haired boy wearing a blue school uniform.

We went to get a cup of coffee at Hayes Hotel and talked for an hour.

"What in God's name were you staring at out there in the middle of the street? He better have been worth it, cuz you almost got yourself killed," Deirdre said.

"He was gorgeous. It was strange. I felt like I had seen him somewhere before, sometime, but I can't remember. I just can't place him." The four of them looked at me like I was a two-headed dog because it was impossible for me to have seen him before. I smiled at them because I knew exactly what they were thinking.

"Ya right Sarah. Maybe in your dreams!" Kiara said laughing. At that moment my heart skipped a beat and I nearly fell of my chair.

Chapter 6

The next morning I had planned to meet the girls just outside the bank at the top of the square at eight thirty-five. Thankfully, I was on time. We arrived at the school around eight forty-five, and as soon as all of the girls were settled in their seats in the classroom, Miss Dwyer came in to speak with us. She explained that we would be studying a unit on Celtic Mythology and she would be coming in to teach us three days a week.

"And, your first class will start right now," Miss Dwyer said. "You don't have to write anything down. You won't be tested. Just listen and enjoy your break from your regular studies."

From that day on, every Tuesday, Wednesday, and Thursday I looked forward to one class in particular. At my other school we of course learned Math, English, Biology and so forth, but there was never anything like Celtic mythology. I was completely intrigued by the magic and mystery of the creatures and ideas from Ireland's past.

"For our first few lessons I will tell you all about the various fairies and creatures, and then I will go on to share stories and myths from the past of our country. Today I want to tell you about Leprechauns," she began. "Now Sarah, I'm sure that many Americans stereotype the Irish and think that there are Leprechauns running around everywhere. However, they are in fact a myth." I laughed because it was true. Many Americans, especially those who were my age, thought that Ireland was made up of drunks, leprechauns, and pots of gold.

Halfway into Miss Dwyer's explanation on the various mannerisms of Leprechauns, I noticed as I looked around the classroom that, with the exception of a few girls, everyone was either asleep on their desks or doing last nights

homework. I was alert and eager to hear more. By the end of the two hours I had learned the real story of Leprechauns. That evening I went home and wrote Sophie a long e-mail.

ೞ ೞ

To: `Polarbear99@aol.com`

From: `Sarbear15@hotmail.com`

Hey girl,

Today was my second day of school. Our class is doing a unit on Celtic Mythology and I learned the truth about the myth of the Leprechaun today! Leprechauns are very old looking men who are often found drunk. However, they can handle their alcohol well so it won't affect their work as shoemakers. They are also guardians of ancient treasures, which they bury in crocks or pots. If a human catches them burying a treasure the Leprechaun will promise them great wealth if he is allowed to go free. I hope I catch one some day! Then Miss Dwyer, the teacher, shared with us the rest of the story and of the idea of catching one of the little guys and becoming rich. It was just too good to be true. They carry two pouches. One contains a silver shilling and a magical coin that always returns to the pouch when it is given out. The other one contains a gold coin, which the Leprechaun will use to bribe his way out of various difficult situations. Unfortunately the gold coin turns into leaves or ashes as soon as it is handed out. In addition to their fooling coins, Leprechauns can disappear in an instant if you divert your eyes for even a second. I've seen a couple short drunk men around since I've been here so I'll make sure to keep my eyes on them!

Love, your world-traveling friend, Sarah

ೞ ೞ

After I sent the e-mail, I heard Jack yell that dinner was ready. Usually, in Ireland dinner is in the middle of the day around one o'clock and tea is in the evening around six o'clock, but since I'm in school during the day, I eat my dinner when I get home from school around three thirty. Jack had made pork chops, potatoes, and peas, and had already begun eating when I entered the kitchen. I joined him at the table and we ate in silence for about two minutes. I wondered about who Jack really was and questioned myself as to why I didn't talk to him more. I mean, if I was going to live with him, I would want to know him. Right as I was opening my mouth to speak he beat me to it.

"Are all the girls treating you all right down there at the school?" he asked.

"Yes, they are all really nice," I told him.

"What about the teachers? Do you have Miss Calloway? She's a right one, isn't she?" he said laughing.

"She's a bit crazy all right. She's my English teacher."

After dinner I helped Jack clean the dishes, then went upstairs to change out of my uniform. I put on a pair of jeans and a light blue hooded sweatshirt along with a pair of white and blue sneakers. I put my hair up into a ponytail, grabbed a bit of change from the nightstand next to my bed and went back downstairs. Jack had moved from the kitchen into a big stuffed chair in the sitting room. He was flicking through the television channels.

"Where you off to?" he asked.

"I'm walking down to Biddy's for a little bit if that's all right," I asked.

"No problem. If it's dark when you're coming home get Paul to give you a lift, alright?"

"Okay, see you later." I said, closing the door behind me. There wasn't much action on the green. There were two little boys riding their bikes around, an old man leaning out over the wall in front of his house, and two girls and a boy sitting on top of a wall about four houses down from Jack's. One of the girls looked vaguely familiar but I couldn't make out her face very well. I had never seen the other girl. The boy hopped off the wall and began hitting a ball back and forth against it. He was using a short wooden stick, quite similar to a field hockey stick except it was much flatter and wider at the bottom. I had to pass them on my way and as I grew closer I clearly recognized the girl because she was in my class at school. She smiled at me and I stopped to properly introduce myself.

"Hey, aren't you in my class at school?" I asked awkwardly, approaching them, "Regina, right?"

"Yea, how are you? I didn't know you were living down here in Childers Park."

"I'm living with my Uncle Jack Ryan," I said as I pointed to our house, number fifty-five.

"Oh, right. Cool. How do you like the school?" she asked.

"It's all right so far I guess." I told her. "I was just on my way down to my grandmother's house, so I'll see you tomorrow," I said, about to walk away.

"Wait," the boy said calling after me. "Are you Nora's and Eoghan's cousin? I go to school with them." I thought for a minute imagining Nora and Eoghan in my head.

"Yes, I am. What's your name?"

"Oh, um, Declan. My name's Declan," he said, twirling the stick around in his hand. He was a bit shorter than me and looked a year younger. He had a round face with big green eyes, and his face was covered in freckles. I thought he was kind of cute.

"Hi, I'm Sarah," I said smiling at him and blushing slightly. He looked so innocent and sweet. "I'll see you around," I said waving to Regina and her friend. I smiled to myself as I was walking away because I knew Declan was still standing there watching me. I looked over my shoulder and he turned and ran back to Regina and her friend.

When I arrived at Biddy's, the yard was filled with commotion. Paul, James, Eoghan, and Bill were tossing around a Rugby ball, Nora was finishing up her work with Twiggy for the evening before she had to go home to do her school work, Eugene was holding Eimear so she could look at one of the horses inside the stables, and Mary's husband, Joe, was in the kitchen eating his dinner. He kept his eyes on his plate and continued to eat. I stood there for a couple of seconds, feeling awkward in the silence, but I eventually walked down the hall where Biddy was just coming out of her bedroom.

"Well Sarah, how are ya?" she asked, surprised to see me standing there.

"I'm pretty good. I started school up at the Presentation on Monday, and I've made a couple of friends," I said. She turned and headed back toward the kitchen. I followed close behind.

"That's great. And how's everyone treating you in Childers Park?" she inquired.

"Fine, everyone is fine. Jack and Una are great to me. They're always trying to feed me," I told her laughing.

"That's what the Irish are like. You'll get used to it." She asked me to go down to the shop for her and buy some Wine Gums. They were her favorite sweets and she was constantly eating them. She gave me some coins from a little leather pouch that she kept in the pocket of the cardigan she wore and told me to get whatever I wanted. On my way out of the

house, I asked Paul if he wouldn't mind giving me a ride home later and he gave me a nod and continued playing ball with the boys. He asked me if I was going to the shop and soon I had orders from him, James and Eoghan. I said goodnight to Nora and Eugene, who were leaving to go home, and I crossed the street to the shop. I came back with Wine Gums for Biddy and chocolate, coke, and crisps for the boys. I grabbed a Cadbury's Golden Crisp chocolate bar for myself. While Biddy and I ate our sweets, Mary arrived home from swimming laps at the pool. She came into the sitting room, followed by Eimear and Bill and joined me on the couch. A second later Joe came in and ordered Bill to get upstairs to get ready for bed because it was nearly eight o'clock. Around nine thirty Paul brought me home. I said "Goodnight" to Jack, who was still in the same spot in front of the T.V. I headed upstairs to my room and watched some T.V. while I tried to fall asleep.

The next morning, I woke up with plenty of time to eat a breakfast of porridge and a cup of tea. I walked a different way to school hoping it would be faster. The girls were already off the bus waiting for me outside the bank. It was Wednesday and I could hardly wait to get to school for our two hours of Celtic Mythology. The girls thought it was strange how interested I was, but they agreed when I said, "It's better than Math or Geography!"

This particular January day in Thurles was quite cold. The wind was fierce, and when it hit my face it stung. Almost every girl who was walking into school that morning was wearing gloves and a hat along with a scarf wrapped tightly around her neck. An over-sized maroon school jacket completed my outfit. In spite of my disgust for the used uniform, jacket, and even scarf the school had "generously" given me, not to mention my hatred for the horrible color combination, I welcomed the layers that warmly bundled me up.

Inside school we created a "strip club". Everyone began peeling off the layers and we were finally able to breathe again. I saw Regina walking in the building with a group of girls whom I didn't recognize, except for her friend from the wall the previous night. When they all parted and she walked into our classroom, I went over to her.

"Hey," I said to her as she ripped off her scarf, hat, and gloves. She continued as if she didn't even notice I was standing in front of her speaking.

"Maybe we can hang out sometime since we live near each other and all," I said, realizing that I was already starting to sound extremely awkward. Finally she looked up to see who it was.

"Oh, Hi Sarah. I didn't know it was you there, I thought it was Maebh and I didn't want to talk to her." She fiddled in her desk for a notebook and a pencil.

"Oh," I laughed. "I know what you mean."

"You should definitely come out around the green after school and on the weekends. Me and the lads are always around," she said.

"Cool, yea I will definitely come out sometime," I said excitedly. Kate, Deirdre, Sinead, Amy, Mairead, and Kiara all lived out towards the countryside, so I was relieved to have a possible friend close to where I was living.

"So, it seemed that Declan had a certain liking for you yesterday, and he'll be out around the green as well ya know, that is, if you're interested," she said with a sly grin on her face. "He's an amazing hurler. Jack's his coach!" She gave me a quick wink and spun around to the front of her desk just as Miss Dwyer entered the room. I had no idea what hurling was but she spun around so quickly I didn't have a chance to ask her. Thankfully I remembered to stay standing, and finally, all at the same time, we sat down in our seats, as directed.

I was distracted for the first half of class as I reviewed what Regina had said. I blushed at the thought of Declan having a crush on me.

Miss Dwyer passed out pictures of the so-called Dullahans and Grogochs. The Dullahans are crazy horsemen who wear black robes. They may be seen riding dark and snorting stallions across the countryside at night. They carry frightening looking heads, which glow in the dark. As the stories became dark and terrifying, very few girls were able to sleep during class. Grogochs, in my opinion, are freaky looking things. They are small old men covered in red hair or fur. They have the power to be invisible and rarely come into sight. However, they are very sociable beings. If a Grogoch trusts you, he will help you. So, however odd they might look with their pointy ears and noses, they actually mean well. Class flew by because all of us found the lecture incredibly interesting. As Miss Dwyer was about to leave the classroom and another teacher was entering, I hopped out of my seat to ask her a quick question.

"Wait, Miss Dwyer. I have a question," I said.

"Yes Sarah?"

"If these creatures are myths, then how are there pictures of them and stories about people seeing them?" I asked, slightly puzzled.

"Well Sarah, you bring up a good point, but as a wise man once said, 'Some say why dream, others say why not'?" She then winked and walked away. For the rest of the week, I was completely and utterly mystified by Miss Dwyer's last words to me. The way she spoke and then winked made me wonder what she was trying to tell me. Was she implying that maybe these myths actually existed? That couldn't be possible. Could it?

Chapter 7

The rest of the week flew by. I never had the chance to go hang out with Regina and her friends because the weather continued to be harsh. After school on Friday, I was on my way home and I caught a glimpse of the gorgeous mystery boy. He was gazing out the window of his bus and before I could be sure it was him, it began to drive off. I realized that I had forgotten to tell Sophie about him or Declan so I decided to go home, make a cup of tea, and write an e-mail about the two boys, both of whom I couldn't seem to get out of my mind. Aisling and Grainne burst in the door of the bedroom and threw their bags on the ground. I had almost forgotten that they would be coming home from college this afternoon.

"Hi, hi, hi, hi, hi! How are you pet? How was the first week of school?" Aisling screamed nearly making me spill my hot tea all over myself.

"Ooo, Daddy told us he saw you talking to Declan the other day," Grainne chimed in. "Oo la, la. He's lovely, Sarah! He plays hurling for Daddy! He's like a son to him. We're friends with his older sisters and we're going to find out if he fancies you!"

"Whoa, whoa, whoa. How many cups of coffee did you two have on the train ride home? Jesus, you've gone mad," I said. "First, school is good. Second, Declan goes to school with Nora and Eoghan and we talked for like a second. Third, what is hurling? And fourth, he's kind of cute. But that's all!" I said laughing and falling into my pillow. Aisling was coyly grinning at me but strangely Grainne had a straight face.

"What's that look for?" I asked her.

"You don't know what hurling is?" she asked as if I should be ashamed of myself. "It's Ireland's national sport for God's sake!"

"Oh, so the wooden stick is used for hurling," I said out loud remembering my confusion the other day.

"We're going to have to bring you to a match, this is just ridiculous. Has your daddy never talked to you about it?"

"No, I guess not."

"All the lads played hurling growing up, I don't know why he never told you. Well, anyways, we're all going to be rooting for you to meet Declan, Daddy too, because he loves the chap," Aisling said getting back to our original conversation.

"I already have met him," I told her.

"No, no," she said laughing at my naivety. "Like kissing him."

"Oh yea. I forgot what that meant," I said laughing at myself.

"Anyways, you comin' out with us tomorrow night? We're just going downtown to the pubs and what not. It will be good crack," Grainne said, confusing me even more. I just smiled and nodded my head because I felt ridiculous asking any more questions. There should be a book or something, like, *Irish Lingo for Beginners.* I thought about what she had just said for a while. Good crack. What did that mean? After I contemplated the statement, and of course didn't get anywhere, Jack called the three of us downstairs for dinner. We had chicken and chips, known to me as French fries. After dinner Grainne, Aisling, and I walked down to Biddy's house. It had been two days since I had been down to see anyone. Unfortunately for me, Declan and a couple of his friends were outside playing hurling on the green. Not that I didn't want to see him, I just feared what Aisling and Grainne would do. As soon as they saw the three of us leaving our yard, they stopped playing and ran over. Thankfully, I looked a lot nicer than the

first time we had met. My hair was down and I had put on make-up after school. He ran over huffing and puffing with sweat beading on his forehead and smiled at me. I smiled back.

"Hey, remember me, we met the other day," I said sounding like a complete idiot. Of course, he wouldn't remember. It wasn't like we went on a date or something.

"How could I forget," he said to my surprise. I couldn't tell whether he was blushing or whether the cold had made his cheeks rosy. "Where you off to?" he asked.

"Oh, just down to my Grandmothers house with Grainne and Aisling." They were standing off to the side talking with the other boys.

"Well, I'm sure I'll be around when you get back," he winked at me and then called to the other boys to keep playing. We walked a great distance without talking so when Grainne and Aisling started rambling on, they hopefully wouldn't hear.

"We don't even have to ask. He fancies you!" they yelped at the same time. I laughed but ignored their comments for the rest of the walk. They walked down to the shop and into the office to see Paul, but I decided to go up to the house. To my surprise, only Biddy was around. Mary must have been off with Nora and the kids somewhere and Joe wasn't home from work yet. Biddy was sitting in her usual spot in the kitchen reading the newspaper and having a cup of tea. I sat down in the seat across the table from her.

"Do you want a cup of tea, Sarah? Or, how about some brown bread? I made it fresh this morning."

"I'm all right. I just ate my dinner down at Jack's house, so I'm stuffed."

"Right, gotcha," she said taking a sip of her tea. "So, any news for me?" she asked.

"Nope, none at all really," I said. "Aisling and Grainne are down at the shop talking to Paul," I told her.

"Oh right. And how is school going for you?" she asked.

"Well actually I really like it. But don't tell anyone," I told her laughing. "I'm learning all about Celtic mythology. It's really interesting."

"Have you learned about the Banshee yet?" Biddy asked, taking her voice down to a low and petrifying tone.

"No, I don't think so, why?" I asked curiously.

"Well," she began, placing her newspaper down on the table, "when I was a child, the boy who lived in the house next to mine went crazy. Nobody knew what had happened, but I knew. I had read about this sort of thing happening in ancient Ireland. One night he snuck out in the middle of the night to follow a piercing wail coming from the fields. He claimed he saw a washerwoman in the middle of the field, covered in blood. He ran home, scared stiff of what he had seen and never spoke about anything else again. He told the same story over and over. He stayed in bed, fearing the banshee. It was horrible. I was a curious child and I read a lot. I also did just what we are doing here. My grandmother told me stories and I learned from them. I was amazed by what I knew had happened that night." I was extremely frightened by what Biddy had just told me. But before I could ask questions Paul, Grainne, and Aisling burst through the door.

"What do you have that look on your face for?" Grainne asked of my wide-eyed jaw-dropped face. I snapped out of it quickly and assured her that nothing was wrong.

"We're going to get a video for tonight," Aisling said. "Want to come along for the ride?"

"No, I'll just trust your judgment to pick a good flick," I told them, and they left.

"Wow, Biddy, is that really true?"

"Only that poor boy knows what he saw and if it was real," she said getting up from her chair and walking towards the hallway door. "I'm wrecked. I'm going to bed. Goodnight."

"Goodnight," I replied.

I realized I didn't feel like watching a movie and decided to start walking back to the park. It wasn't quite dark yet, so I knew it would be fine if I walked home. I thought about the banshee the whole way home and grew to be incredibly frightened. When I was nearly at the house, I felt a hand on my shoulder. My heart skipped a beat and I let out an enormous scream.

"Sarah." I turned around to see that Declan had run after me. "Are you all right?"

"Jesus, you nearly scared me to death. What are you doing?"

"Not much at all," he said looking deep into my eyes. "Want to take a walk?"

I was unsure if it was a smart idea because I didn't know him at all, but he seemed harmless, so I agreed.

"Let me catch my breath for a second," I said leaning on the wall. We hopped over a small stonewall that separated the backs of the houses from a field.

"So, how are you liking Thurles so far?" he said trying to make conversation with me.

"I like it a lot. I love my family here and everything."

"That's good." We walked in silence for a while. When he finally started talking again he asked me all about America. He seemed genuinely interested in me. He wondered where I was from and what it was like.

"It's so different from Ireland. The school is different, the people are different, the whole way of life is different," I tried to explain to him. "The school is more formal. The people are more natural and welcoming. Life seems more balanced with time out of doors, time to talk with family, and time to be with friends. Well..what about you? Who exactly is Declan?"

"Well let's see, here's my life in a nutshell," he began. I watched him talk. The way his mouth moved and the words rolled off his tongue made this foreign accent that I sometimes didn't even understand. "I go to school at the Christian Brothers, I play Hurling, I've got two older sisters and a younger brother, I like to go out on the weekends with the lads, and I hate Brussels sprouts. That's my life summed up for you," he said. I laughed at the Brussels sprouts comment. "Now you go," he said, implying that I now had to sum up my life for him.

"Okay," I said. "I go to the Presentation School and I don't play any sports. I like to read, and I like to write. My favorite colors are orange, green, and pink. I love chocolate, especially Cadbury. I now love to travel. I have three best friends at home and I do everything with them. I have one older sister Morgan who is already off in college, and I was incredibly bored in Syracuse, New York, where I'm from and decided that I needed a change. So, here I am. Oh, and by the way, I don't care for Brussels sprouts either," I said laughing. I looked up and he was smiling at me. "And there, Declan, is my life in a nut shell. It's extremely boring and dull. Ta da!"

"No, no, no. Not at all. You're far from dull," he said. I looked up and studied his face. I had no idea what time it was, but I did know it was late.

"Oh crap! I've got to go. I'll see you tomorrow. I'm going to go out with Aisling and Grainne tomorrow night. Maybe I'll see you," I said as I started running across the fields. Declan watched out for me as I reached the wall, hopped over and

made it to the house. I decided to catch my breath before I went inside so that Jack wouldn't question me. He was in his chair in the sitting room. I knew, because I could hear the television. I walked by the door and tried to bolt upstairs to the bedroom.

"Sarah? Is that you?" I heard Jack call out to me before I even made it to the second step. I went into the sitting room and plopped down on the couch.

"Hi, Jack! What are you watching?"

"Oh, just some special on The History Channel. So... what do you think of Declan. He's a nice chap, isn't he? He plays hurling for the team I coach. He's like a son to me," he said, pretending to be just making basic conversation. I decided that I would play along.

"Oh, um, sure! I guess. He's nice."

"Well, do you like him?" I guess he gave up quickly on the basic conversation and decided to jump right in and be forward with me.

"I mean he's nice," I said. "I hardly know him."

"Well, I think you should get to know him. He came to talk to me tonight after you girls went down to Biddy's. He asked me about you and I told him you would go to the cinema with him sometime or something. I told him you were a bit shy but he should chat you up a bit."

"Oh, okay. Thanks Jack," I said feeling completely unthankful.

"Well that's all I wanted to say," he said. I left the room confused by what had just happened. Did my uncle honestly get me a date? Not to sound ungrateful, but why would he do that? I wondered. That night I couldn't sleep because my head was filled with thoughts. I was thinking about Biddy's story

and what Jack had done. I knew that if I fell asleep, my dreams would not be pleasant.

When I woke up the next morning, I remembered that my dreams were in fact unpleasant. I ignored my terrifying dream about the banshee and my dream of having an awkward date to the movies with Declan. As the day went on I was more and more excited for the night because I would be going out with Aisling and Grainne to see real Thurles nightlife. Around six o'clock the room was filled with commotion. Clothes flew from dresser drawers and the wardrobe, blow dryers wailed, and eyelashes were curled. Aisling, Grainne, and I were getting ready for a night on the town. After convincing Aisling to take a risk and wear a red shirt, we allowed a compromise and let her wear black pants. She wore flat, tan, suede boots. She had straightened her hair and was wearing it down with a side part. Grainne had chosen a pair of jeans and a dark turquoise top, along with turquoise earrings and black pointed toe boots. She also had her hair straightened and in a side part. I chose to wear my favorite pair of jeans, the ones that always made me feel fabulous, a pair of black pointed toe boots, and a simple long sleeved black top. Once we were finally ready to leave, after pampering and beautifying ourselves, we went downstairs to say goodbye to Jack and Una.

"You take care of her, girls," he sternly told Aisling and Grainne.

"Geez Da, what do you think we'd do with her? Let her off downtown and tell her good luck?" Grainne cried.

"All right. Well! we're off," Aisling said.

"I'll see you tomorrow," I said to Jack and Una.

"Be safe!" Una shouted as we were on our way out the door.

We walked through the town, past the many pubs that were already filled with music. Outside many of the fast food

restaurants, younger kids hung out with friends, munching on chips and burgers. We made our way down to a pub called the County, where Aisling and Grainne's friends were, including James and Paul. The place was packed. You couldn't move a muscle without knocking someone's drink or stepping on someone's toes. We made our way to the back of the pub, right next to the bathrooms. Paul and James stood chatting with three other guys. Grainne and Aisling each grabbed a seat and I began to introduce myself to all the people staring at me like I had two heads. The boys talking to Paul and James were named Larry, Emmit, and Gary. All three of them were extremely cute; tall, rugged, and with accents that no American female could resist. However, they were much older than me, but a girl can dream, right? At the table, in order of introduction sat many of Aisling and Grainne's girlfriends, but I couldn't hear their names over the loud music. Bad luck for me. Two of the girls were Declans' older sisters, who tried giving me the third degree. I kept my mouth shut for fear of anything getting back to Declan. While Grainne and Aisling chatted with their friends I stood with James and we talked.

"So, any news? How was your first week at school?" he asked.

"No, not really. It was good…" I said trying to contribute to the conversation the best I could. "Do you know Declan O'Neil?"

"Yup. I know him. He goes to school with Eoghan. He lives in the park. Why, do you fancy him?"

"Shhhhh," I warned him so Declan's sisters wouldn't hear us talking. "No, I don't fancy him, but Uncle Jack likes him and set me up on a date with him!"

"Give him a chance," James said, laughing at me. He turned to Paul to tell him the story. Of course, Paul instantly joined in the laughter and the two of them started to make fun of me.

Seeing that Aisling and Grainne weren't doing the best job of "watching" over me, I went to the bathroom without telling them. After I had used the bathroom and washed my hands, I stood in front of the sink for at least five minutes. I thought about Declan. He was a really nice person but what if it turned out I didn't like him as more than a friend in the end? How would I tell him? And for that matter, how would I tell Jack? I decided to head back out into the crowd. I opened the bathroom door and standing, with his back to me, was the one and only Declan. He was talking to Aisling, Grainne, and his two sisters, and as soon as they spotted me, they started screaming.

"Oh look! There she is, Declan! We've been looking for you Sarah!" Aisling screamed over the music. Declan turned around and flashed me a smile. I looked over and saw James pointing at me laughing. He knew I was uncomfortable, but he wanted to torture me. I decided that I had to be polite and talk with Declan because everyone was expecting me to be in love with him. I grabbed his hand and dragged him over to the opposite side of the bar where there were two empty stools. I assured Aisling and Grainne that I wouldn't leave the pub to run off with Declan; it was just that I needed to sit down. He politely asked me if I wanted something to drink, but I declined. I had finished my Diet Coke a while ago and was refreshed. He scooted his chair closer to mine so we could hear each other clearly. In the beginning it was awkward, while we worked through the normal small talk, but after a while we drifted into deep conversation. I found it so easy to talk to him because there was something so comforting and laid back. "I miss my friends back home," I said. "It's not that there's no one to talk to here, but I miss people who have known me for a long time. I even miss my parents."

"That's one of the great things about living in Thurles. Everyone knows you and most have know you since you were born. They might know your father or even your grandfather.

I think if I had to move or travel to a new place I'd feel invisible. I could never do what you've done, Sarah," Declan responded.

Apparently we were so caught up in conversation that time had flown by. It was midnight already and the pub was closing. Crowds of people were heading across the street to the nightclub. I lost Declan in the crowd but luckily I walked in with Paul and his friend Gary, and we were not carded. I technically didn't feel I was doing anything wrong. Yes, I was under age but I wasn't drinking. I was just having a good time. When we were inside, Paul, who had already had a few pints of Guinness, whisked me onto the dance floor. This place was also packed. There was a huge dance floor surrounded by three different bars and some places to sit. Paul and I were lost in the crowd. I laughed at his goofy dance moves. We looked like complete lunatics, but neither of us cared.

Three dances later I needed a break. I grabbed some random girl and forced her to take over my position. Of course, Paul barely noticed. I ventured over to where Aisling was talking with some guy.

"Hey Hun!" she yelled excitedly. When she spoke she came extremely close to my face and I could practically taste the alcohol off her breath. I waved my hand in front of my face in hopes that she would get the hint.

"Are you having a good time?" she asked backing slightly away from me.

"Yea, I am. Paul can really dance," I said sarcastically.

She started laughing, "I know isn't he a hoot!" Just then I felt a hand on my shoulder and a voice whisper into my ear.

"Dance with me?" I spun around to see who it was. Declan of course. Aisling lost her balance and fell into me, leading to a domino effect. Declan caught me in his arms and then dragged

me back onto the dance floor. We danced very close to one another and I could feel his heart beating against my chest. I flirted with him while we danced, just for fun. He was cute but there was something missing. I didn't feel the "zing". We danced for multiple songs, with slow and fast beats. He looked into my eyes. He told me he saw something in me that he had never seen in anyone before. During a slower song I rested my head on his shoulder and he rocked me back and forth. I wanted this to be special. Could wanting something make it happen?

Straight ahead, I noticed a familiar face. I looked closer. It was the mystery boy, and he was talking to my cousin James. I caught myself staring at him and quickly turned away, but I wasn't fast enough. He saw me and gave me a slight smile. I wished I could have gone to him to find out his name, but I couldn't do that to Declan. I felt something so strange and unusual for him, and I didn't even know his name.

At three o'clock in the morning, on our way back to Childers Park, Grainne and Aisling acted like drunken fools, laughing at everything they saw. Around each corner and in front of each pub stood little, old, drunk men, talking nonsense of wealth and money. Every time I saw one of these men, whether they were having a smoke, or stumbling home, or wandering aimlessly around the town, I couldn't help but wonder if maybe, just maybe, they were Leprechauns.

Chapter 8

February was a cold month in Thurles. One extremely frosty day, when we were sitting in class, it began to snow. I noticed the first flakes falling as I gazed out the window, but it didn't mean anything to me. In Syracuse, we get an intense amount of snow each winter, but in Ireland, even one snowfall is rare. The excitement on the girls' faces made me smile inside and, even though the snow only stuck for a few hours, we had a lot of fun during break and lunch, collecting enough snow for one or two snowballs to throw at each other and catching flakes with our mouths and feeling them melt on our tounges.

After school was out that day the square was filled with excited children and teens having snowball fights and enjoying the unexpected snow flakes. As snowballs were flying overhead, Kate, Deirdre, and I walked around the square, weaving in and out of stores. We finally decided to get a cup of tea and warm up a bit, before facing the cold again. On our way inside, I spotted the boy.

"There he is! There he is!" I shouted, grabbing Kate and Deirdre's arms.

"There who is?" Deirdre asked, scamming the crowded square for whoever I was pointing at.

"Oh, your guy! The mystery boy!" Kate exclaimed. I had my eyes on him as if I was a lion and he was my prey so I wouldn't lose him in the crowd. Just as I was pointing again to show the girls, a snowball hit me smack in the face. I wiped the snow off my face and turned around to see Eoghan and Declan standing there and fully prepared to strike again.

"Damn! I lost him." I said, extremely disappointed. I was so frustrated with Eoghan and Declan who distracted me from the beautiful boy whose name I didn't even know, I knelt down on the ground, grabbed a handful of snow and threw it at Declan.

When they both began to attack, I ducked, forcing the snowballs to hit Kate and Deirdre. The girls had the most shocked looks on their faces. Soon the five of us were in a snowball war, running, screaming, and falling all over the place dodging a hit to the head or getting a good aim at someone else. When we finally called it quits almost all the snow in the square had melted away. I properly introduced Kate and Deirdre to Eoghan and Declan and they joined us for a cup of tea. Two cups of tea and a scone later Kate leaned in close to me and whispered. "Declan is so cute. Find out if he's interested, will you?" I wasn't surprised that she liked him.

A couple of minutes later, Kate and Deirdre left to go and catch their bus and Eoghan headed off home. Declan and I started walking back to the Park in the piercing cold. We were just outside of his house when I finally decided to ask him about Kate.

"So, what do you think of Kate?"

"She's nice. Why?"

"No, what do you *think* of her? Do you think she's pretty? Would you meet her?" I asked, hoping he would catch on this time.

"Oh, I get it. Um, I don't think so, Sarah," he said turning to walk towards his front door. "I'll see you tomorrow."

As I walked the rest of the way to my house I wondered whether he honestly had no interest in Kate or whether he still hadn't moved on from me. I secretly hoped it was that he had no interest in Kate although I would never tell her that. I didn't know what I would say to her to explain why Declan didn't like her.

I came home to find Jack and Una both gone and my dinner on a plate on the stove. Una arrived home about twenty minutes after I did and Jack followed another half hour later. Una said that she had had to work late, and I realized that so far I had

had no idea what she did. To my surprise she worked at the convent down at the church and took care of many of the nuns, mostly cooking their meals. I told her that a couple of the nuns worked at my school but none of them was my teacher.

That night I called home to talk with my parents. My mother answered the phone and sounded thrilled to talk to me.

"Mom you would love my favorite class! It's all about mythological creatures of Ireland. I'm more and more interested each week!"

"That's great, Honey!" she said. "Oh, I almost forgot. I saw your girlfriends the other night at the video store. They all say hello and they miss you very much, as do your father and I."

"I miss all of you, too! Wow! I'd completely forgotten to tell you how much I miss girls' night," I said, suddenly realizing that I missed my friends terribly. As I finished talking to my mom, my dad came on the phone.

"I can't believe I waited this long to meet this family. They're all amazing, Dad," I told him trying not to make him too jealous that he wasn't here. "I've become really close with Biddy. She tells me all about the myths that she knows from the past."

"That's great that she tells you. She hardly ever shares deep secrets with anyone," he said sounding surprised. "I hope she's not telling you any lies about me!"

"Oh, she's told me plenty about you and your brothers' mischievous behavior as kids," I said laughing. After chatting for just a short while, I heard my mother yelling in the background, "International calls aren't cheap!"

After I hung up,I went into the sitting room where Jack was already in his usual spot watching some program on wild animals in Africa. I sat down on the couch next to his chair. He quickly reached down and passed me a tin of biscuits he was eating. I smiled at him because he always had little

nighttime treats somewhere in the room. I took a couple of chocolate-covered ones and handed the tin back. Every other day I would join him in the sitting room to have an update of our lives and we would do this same biscuit ritual over again, although the television program varied. He asked me about school, my friends, how I liked living in Thurles. Then he would try to sneak in a little comment about Declan. He always hoped he could trick me into answering and then continue on with the conversation.

"So, how are things going?" he asked, keeping his eyes on the T.V.

"Fine, everything's fine."

"That's good. How's Declan? Are you two getting on okay? How's school?"

"School is fine as well," I said, laughing inside because I had pretended I didn't hear the two middle comments. But, of course, he would not back down. He was determined to talk about Declan, and because I eventually gave in, he had exactly what he wanted.

"I was talking to him the other day while I was out in the garden. He told me you didn't seem very interested in him, but of course you are, right? So anyways, you're going to the movies on Friday night. It'll be fun. He's a nice chap."

I rolled my eyes out of complete annoyance for what Jack had done. Unfortunately, I wasn't in a place with Jack yet where I could go off in a ranting rage about how angry I was at him for doing such a stupid thing. He looked at me blankly hoping I would respond to his statement in some way. I smiled politely and rose up from the couch to leave. I stopped short, turned around to give him a piece of my mind but then I sighed and decided I didn't have the courage. I grabbed a handful of biscuits and quietly, but not contentedly, I left the room.

I went upstairs to get ready for bed. I was worn out but decided to write three letters before going to sleep. I wrote one to Sophie, one to Hailey, and one to Taylor because I hadn't spoken to any of them in what seemed like an eternity. I desperately needed to fill them in and hear all the gossip from back home in return. Sophie would be curious to hear about what everything looked like and what was really different from home. Taylor would be completely engrossed in my Declan and my mystery man dilemma, and she would definitely have advice for me. Hailey would be most concerned with my home life, making sure that living with Jack and Una was all right. She would also be concerned about my new friends, making sure I had made some, that they were nice, and that they weren't as good as my three best ones on the other side of the ocean. After I finished filling them in on my life, my hand hurt. Plus, I could barely keep my eyes open.

The next day I woke up late and didn't get to the square early enough to meet the girls. I did get to school just in time to beat the first teacher to the classroom. Kiara passed a note over to me during first period that read:

All of us girls are going to sleep at my house on Friday night! I'll fill you in on the details later!

I looked up to see all of them smiling with excitement; however, my expression stayed dull and apathetic. Friday night was my "date" with Declan, and I didn't know how I was going to explain that I couldn't sleep at Kiara's, especially to Kate, who was going to be devastated. Just as I was caught up in my moment of distress, I received another note. It was from Kate.

So, what did he say? Does he fancy me? Give him my number!

087 534267

I didn't respond to either of the notes and I waited until break to reply to both. During the next two classes I concocted the

best lie I could think of as my excuse for not being able to go to Kiara's on Friday night. Then I would do my best to persuade Declan to go to the movies on Saturday night instead. I decided to say I had to mind my two little cousins for my aunt. As for my excuse for why Declan didn't like Kate, I was absolutely doomed.

Kate ran over to me quickly the minute break began and started throwing questions all over the place. I waited while she calmed down and said the first thing that came to mind.

"He likes someone else, but he wouldn't tell me who," I blurted out feeling horrible for Kate and for lying. "I'm really sorry, Kate." I think she was more shocked than anything, and before she could respond Kiara came over to talk about Friday night.

"Okay so I'm going to buy loads of sweets and crisps. Deirdre is getting videos, and you can just bring your gorgeous little self!" she yapped eagerly.

"I'm really sorry Kiara, but I already told my aunt I'd mind my two little cousins for her Friday night."

"Damn! Well, we can't have it Saturday because Sinead and Amy both have to work. Aw, well. Maybe next time." I felt overwhelmed with guilt and desperately needed chocolate. I grabbed Colleen's arm and we went into the cafeteria to get doughnuts. I indulged and ate two!

We had gym class next. I was glad because I needed to run off some steam, not to mention my need to leave behind the hefty number of calories I consumed during break. After gym, we had mythology. Miss Dwyer introduced us to a very interesting fairy.

"This particular fairy is called a Puck, and he is extremely different from the other ones I have told you about," she began to explain. "I guess you could consider him a trickster, although his actions are accidental." She passed around some

pictures. It was a simple looking fairy; pretty much what one would assume a fairy to look like, a small man with wings that glowed in the light of the moon.

"They usually try to help make situations better, but mostly end up making them worse," Miss Dwyer continued. "They are often servants of other important mythological creatures,who order their Puck to make something happen. In the end, it plays out in a confusing and mixed up way."

For the rest of the class we read different stories and scenarios aloud. These included one where a puck was ordered to turn a criminal into a pig and bring endless happiness to a man the criminal had harmed. The Puck found the two men; however, from a distance he confused them and the criminal was granted eternal happiness, while the other man was turned into a pig. The Puck's master scorned him for making such a mess. The Puck righted everything in the end by using more magic.

After school, I decided to avoid the girls and head straight home. As I walked through the square, en route to Childers Park, I spotted Declan walking alone. I starting running toward him shouting his name until I finally drew his attention.

"Declan, I need to talk to you! Wait up!" I yelled looking like a lunatic running through the streets. He heard me and turned around. He let me catch my breath before we started talking.

"Look, Sarah. If it's about Kate again-" he began. "I'm just really not interested."

"Actually it's not about Kate. It's about the cinema Friday night."

"Oh, okay? Are you going to give me some excuse-?"

"No, actually," I said interrupting him. "I was wondering if we could go on Saturday night."

"Sure, that's fine."

"Great!" We walked together the rest of the way home ,and although there was a slight chill, the sun was peeking out from behind a cloud, warming our faces. We both went to change out of our uniforms and agreed to meet back outside at four o'clock. I put on a pair of jeans and a green wool sweater. It was sunny, but it was still the middle of February. I sat down with Jack to eat dinner and then told him I was going to embrace the nice weather while I could. Declan was walking toward my house right as I walked out the door.

"Perfect timing," I said. He smiled and we walked over to where Regina and some other people were sitting. I noticed that Declan was holding two hurling sticks, and I asked him why he had brought them both out.

"To teach you how to play!" he said, tossing the ball up in the air and hitting it across the green to where another boy was standing with a stick. It bounced off his stick and into the air a couple times before he caught it in his hand and prepared to hit it back toward Declan and me. It landed a couple of feet in front of me. Declan picked it up and showed me how to bounce it on the stick.

"It's all about balance. Then when you get the hang of that, you toss the ball in the air and hit it."

"Oh, yea, I get it. It is just that simple," I said sarcastically. He handed me one of the sticks and the ball. I tossed the ball into the air and swung the stick. I completely missed the ball and swung the stick around. Luckily, Declan was expecting me to do that so he had prepared to duck and avoid a head injury. I turned around. Regina and three other girls were hysterically laughing, as well as Declan himself. I dropped the stick and proclaimed, "I give up!"

I went over and sat down on the wall next to Regina and she introduced me to her friends.

"That's Marie, Lesley, and Carrie," she said, pointing to them one by one.

"Hey, I'm Sarah."

After hours of chatting and a couple of more tries at hurling, it started getting dark and I headed inside.

"See you tomorrow, lads," I said opening the gate to my yard and realizing that I had just sounded totally Irish by saying lads!

The next morning, Kiara and the rest of the girls were thrilled when I informed them that I could come on Friday night.

The rest of the week went by fast and Friday came before we knew it. I convinced Paul to give me a ride out to Kiara's house that night and Kate said her mom would give me a ride home in the morning. I packed a bag of things before Paul came to pick me up – two photo albums of my friends and family back home, some CDs, some American candy my mom had sent over in a package for me, and my two full bags of make-up.

I was the last to arrive because I lived the farthest from Kiara's house. I was really excited because this is exactly what my friends and I did at home, and I was beginning to really miss it.

"Hey, everybody!" I said excitedly when I entered the room where everyone was awaiting my arrival.

"Hey, Sarah!" they shouted at the same time.

We ate, watched movies, did makeovers, and talked about school, friends, and boys all night long. We talked about embarrassing moments, sad moments and all the memorable moments in our lives.

"So what's so special about this guy, Sarah?" Amy asked.

"I have no idea! I have only seen him from a distance and I don't even know his name but I feel like I'm in love with him."

"That's utterly impossible. You're just completely infatuated with him!" Sinead exclaimed.

"I don't know. There's something else. I have to meet him." All night long, we asked each other questions. The next morning, when we finally rose from our beds, we knew so much more about each other. I had confessed my love for a boy I didn't even know and now we were determined to find out his name. I promised Kate I would do my best to work on Declan for her and I told Kiara I would talk to my cousin James for her. We learned, we laughed, and I think we even may have cried.

As soon as I arrived home on Saturday afternoon, I immediately went back to bed. We had stayed up so late, or early, that I was extremely tired and decided I had to take a nap so I didn't fall asleep during the movie later that night. I woke up from my nap at five o'clock and went downstairs for dinner. I had left to go to Kiara's early the previous day and hadn't seen Grainne or Aisling, and they were in the kitchen. I joined in the cooking and the steak and potatoes was ready that little bit faster. After dinner, I showered and the girls insisted on helping me get ready for my "big date". Yea, right!

I decided on a pair of jeans, a pair of brown pointy toe flats, and a brown sweater. It was cold and yet nice out, but I figured I'd better bring a jacket, just in case. Grainne and Aisling piled on the make-up, insisted on straightening my hair, and drenched me in perfume. Finally, at seven thirty, Declan arrived at that house so we could walk down to the movie theater. I snuck out before Jack insisted on taking a picture or giving Declan the *If anything happens to her I've got a gun in the back* speech. Declan wore a pair of brown corduroy pants, a navy blue long sleeved shirt and a pair of boat shoes. At the theater, he insisted on buying my ticket, so I bought the popcorn and the sweets. He picked two seats in the middle of the theater where nobody was sitting.

"So, just to get things straight. Is this a date?" he asked ,seeming embarrassed but eager to hear my answer.

"Um, Yea, I guess. I mean we're friends, but we're at the movies together, so yea, I guess it's a date."

"Oh," he said, sounding completely shut down and disappointed by the word "friend." He continued eating his popcorn and stared at the blank movie screen while we silently waited for *Troy* to begin. I felt horrible, but I had to make it clear to him that we were friends. During the movie, there were couples cuddling and kissing all around us, which just made our situation worse. All the same, I felt extremely comfortable with him. After the movie, we walked down to the square where Regina, Marie, Carrie, Lesley and a bunch of other people from the Park were hanging out. Regina and the girls questioned me about my date with Declan but I assured them we were just friends. I explained that "the feeling" was missing and, of course, they understood completely. If I tried to explain that to Declan, he would probably turn his head like a confused puppy, but all girls understood what I meant.

Two sodas and two burgers later, Declan walked me home. He held my hand, and I let him. In front of my gate, I kissed him goodnight on the cheek and went inside. I would eventually explain that all I wanted was a friendship, but now was not the time, especially if Jack was watching. Jack practically had our wedding date picked out. I tiptoed upstairs, brushed my teeth and quietly went to bed.

Chapter 9

As another month passed, the weather grew less harsh and the sun began to shine quite a bit more. It was the first day in April, and as I walked to school, the sun was beginning to peek out from behind one of the only clouds in sight. Kiara ran up to me as I entered the school and started jumping up and down. "My aunty in Dublin invited me up for a weekend! She said I could bring my friends as well! You have to come! Will you? Please! Please!"

"Oh, my god! That would be great!" I said, just as excited.

"I know! Me, You, Kate, and Deirdre are going in three weeks! We're pretty much just gonna shop and then we can show you around Dublin a bit! It'll be right crack!" She grabbed my hand and dragged me into the classroom where Kate and Deirdre sat together talking and awaiting my answer.

"She's coming, lads!" Kiara shouted as the two of them jumped up elatedly.

"Well, I have to make sure it's all right with my Uncle Jack but I'm sure it'll be fine!" I said, thrilled that they had even thought to invite me. "Oh crap. I just realized, I have no money to buy a train ticket or go shopping up there," I told them, feeling slightly embarrassed and very disappointed.

They looked embarrassed and disappointed too, but before they could respond, a nun entered the room.

"All right girls, chat time is over! Get to your seats! Miss McCormick is out for the day so I'm watching over the class. You can either read or work quietly for first period."

I chose to sit silently and pretend to work. I thought about my options to earn some quick cash. Unfortunately, nothing

instantly popped into my head, because basically I had no ideas. I couldn't call home and ask for money because my mother probably wouldn't even want me to go, not to mention they didn't have any money to send to me; it was enough to save up the money for the ticket over here. The girls passed me notes with various options throughout the class period.

To: Sarah

From: Kiara

> What about getting a job at one of the shops in town or something?

To: Kiara

From: Sarah

> No one will hire me. I'm not a citizen.

To: Sarah

From: Deirdre

> What about if you mind your cousins for your aunty?

To: Deirdre

From: Sarah

> I can't do that. They've been so nice to me! I couldn't ask her to pay me.

To: Sarah

From: Kate

> Would your Uncle lend you the money? You could do work around the house to pay him back.

To: Kate

From: Sarah

> I don't know. I mean I should be doing work around the house anyway. He *is* letting me live there after all.

To: Kiara, Deirdre, and Kate

From: Sarah

Thanks for the suggestions girls but I think it's a lost cause. ☹

For the rest of the day, the four of us acted slightly depressed. I desperately wanted to go and they desperately wanted me to go as well. After school I went home and moped in my room. It would be so much fun to go to Dublin with the girls. I would get to shop and see the sights. After a long sulking session in my room, and after missing dinner, I decided to walk down to Biddy's. Thankfully, when I left the house, nobody was around the green. I was in no mood to speak to Declan right now or to explain to him why I seemed upset. I knew he would ask. When I strolled up the driveway, no one was in the yard, but I did see Nora up on her horse trotting around the arena. She looked so graceful when she rode. She was so in sync with the horse and they moved in motion together. I opened the door to the kitchen where Biddy, Eugene, Mary, Bill, and Eimear all sat at the table eating their supper. They casually looked up, greeted me, and continued eating. Biddy, however, noticed something was wrong by the look on my face. I insisted that nothing was wrong but I apparently couldn't fool her.

"Well, I guess there is this one thing," I began.

"Ah ha! I knew it!" she exclaimed happily.

"A girl in my class invited me up to Dublin for a night to stay with her aunt and I really want to go."

"You should go. There's loads to do up in Dublin," Mary chimed in.

"Well you see, I would love to go, but… I have no money for a train ticket, or for anything else I would do up there," I explained. "And I can't get a job here because I'm not a citizen, and I can't call home for any money because, well, we

simply don't have any." Biddy and Mary stared at me with consideration for a moment, and Eugene continued to enjoy his meal. After a couple of more minutes of silence Biddy was sure she had come up with the best idea.

"Eugene will give you a job!" she loudly proclaimed. Eugene lifted one eye up toward Biddy and me. He smiled slightly. "You were just telling me how you were short of staff for that big wedding coming up!"

I smiled widely as he thought about the idea.

"I'm a really hard worker. I won't let you down!" I yelped. "I promise."

"Well, I don't know," Eugene, said, still pondering the idea.

"Oh come on Eug, give her the job," Mary insisted.

"All right," he said continuing his meal.

"Yes! Thank you so so much!" I exclaimed. "You don't know how much this means to me!"

"Great. Well that settles that," Biddy said smacking her hand down on the table as though she was completely satisfied with herself. She got up to head toward the sitting room where she could have peace and quiet and watch the telly.

After he had finished eating Eugene said, "Come down on Wednesday night so the other girls can show you how everything is done. If you can handle it, you can work the rest of the week and then the wedding is this weekend."

"Oh, shut up Eugene. The girl can handle it. She's a Ryan for Christ's sake!" Biddy called out on her way down the hallway to the sitting room.

Since I knew the money part was covered, I next had to make sure that the trip was okay with Jack. I thanked Eugene numerous times before rushing out the door to get home. I

waved to Biddy as I passed the sitting room window. As I approached the green, I passed Declan who was sitting in front of his house with two girls I didn't recognize but I ran right past them. At the house Una was in her spot in the kitchen and Jack in his spot in the sitting room. I went in to sit down with Jack to beg him to let me go to Dublin.

"Hey, Jack!"

"Hello Sarah. How was your day at school?" he asked, staying focused on the telly as usual.

"It was great. Actually, Kiara asked me if I would go to Dublin with her and two other girls and stay with her aunt for a night. Would you let me go?"

"I guess I have no problem with that," he said. I was worried. He said yes so quickly and calmly without asking any questions. Was this to good to be true? I decided to go with it.

"Really? Thanks you so much. I really want to go but I was worried you wouldn't want me to travel to Dublin. Thank you!" I said jumping off the couch to give him a hug.

"I mean we will have to figure a few things out but that sounds all right with me," he said. "Oh wait, there's one more thing. How do you plan on paying for your train ticket?"

"I'm one step ahead of ya. Eugene offered me a job at the restaurant. Isn't that great?" I said ecstatically. I left the room and shut the door behind me. I couldn't believe he said yes, and I couldn't wait till school the next day to tell the girls that I could go. I fell asleep that night with a smile planted on my face.

I practically sped through my morning routine and ran all the way to the bank where I met the girls in the morning. I stood there fidgeting and antsy waiting for their bus to arrive. As soon as the girls were off the bus they could tell I had news.

"I can go! I'm going to Dublin! Jack said yes, and my Uncle Eugene is giving me a job at his restaurant."

"Yay!" they screamed in unison. They jumped off the bus and we had a big group hug before heading off to school. Throughout the day the girls told me all the different places they were going to take me to in Dublin and about all the great shops. I was so excited to start working in the restaurant and to finally have some money.

When Wednesday rolled around, I couldn't wait to go to work. I changed into black pants, a black shirt, and black shoes at Biddy's and arrived at the restaurant around four o'clock. I walked through the shop and in the back entrance to the restaurant. A man who I assumed to be the chef was standing in the kitchen getting organized for the night.

"Hi, I'm Sarah, Eugene's niece. I'm starting work tonight."

"Oh great. Welcome. Nice to meet you," he said as I continued on through the kitchen and into the bar area of the restaurant.

"My name's Aiden by the way." He was not too tall but not too short. He had short dark hair and was in bad need of a shave. He wore black cotton pants and a white chef's jacket. He had a round figure and a large belly, but who could blame him, he did cook food all day. The restaurant was decorated with green and yellow walls, light wooden tables and chairs, and large potted plants about every five feet. The bar was fully stocked with liquor, beers, and wines. There was a coffee maker, two beers taps, and a mini fridge, which contained sodas and beers. Just in front of the bar was the waiting area, which had cushioned benches and chairs. I stood back to admire my new work place when two girls pushed open the sliding doors and entered the restaurant. They were wearing similar outfits to mine and I assumed them to be the other two waitresses.

"Hi, I'm Sarah, Eugene's niece-"

"No need for introductions. He told us all about you," the girl on the right said.

"We'll take care of you and show you the ropes. It's a piece of cake," the other one said.

"Great! Thanks," I said happy to be able to skip the explanation of who I was and what I was doing there.

"I'm Catriona and this is Carolyn." She was short and chubby and had a very friendly and inviting smile; however, she didn't have the greatest teeth. Carolyn was about the same height and weight as Catriona and was very well groomed.

"We'd better get started right away," Carolyn said. First they showed me how to set the tables and properly fold the napkins. They showed me the key to the door and how to correctly clean the glasses. We also had to sweep and mop the floors. It was five o'clock by the time we had finished all that. They then showed me how to use the coffee maker and make proper breadbaskets for the tables. I learned the various drinks and I was told to study the menu and wine list. Unfortunately, since I was the rookie, I cleaned the bathrooms, but I didn't mind. I was just thankful I had a job. Just before people were starting to arrive, they filled me in on last minute details like the music, the beer taps, and the flower/candle centerpieces that were placed on each table. I was extremely nervous and I knew I would forget something, but they assured me I would be fine. When the first couple came through the door, Carolyn handed me a pen and an order booklet and sent me to get drink orders. I happily greeted the couple and asked them to sit down while they browsed through the menu, and just as Catriona had taught me, I asked them if they were interested in having a drink before dinner. I headed back to the bar with an order for vodka and tonic and a pint of Guinness. I let the two girls make the drinks and I watched closely. As more parties

came in, Catriona and Carolyn said that the first couple was the only table I had to worry about for the night. At times I was confused and slightly disheveled, but I made it through the night without dropping anything or messing up an order. It was a quiet night and everyone left by ten o'clock. The three of us cleaned up, locked the door and headed home. I decided to walk even though it was dark because I was hot from rushing around the restaurant. I slept soundly, exhausted from the first night of work; however, I could hardly wait until the next day.

On Thursday and Friday night at the restaurant, I began to notice customers more than I noticed the work. I wasn't slacking on being a good waitress, but I started to really observe the mannerisms of different people who dined at the restaurant. One man caught my attention. Judging by his hair color and the look of his skin, about sixty. He came in with three other men on Thursday night, the other three all much younger. They sat in front of the bar for some time, drinking and having a laugh. I first took their drink orders. After that, each time I went back to check on them, I noticed that Dr. Spain's hands were shaking slightly. I watched him pick his glass of whiskey off the table and as he lifted it to his lips the ice in the glass rattled as his hand shook uncontrollably. When I came again at the table to take their orders, I noted that they picked and chose from the menu one by one. Dr. Spain ordered the duck.

"Darlin', Will you ask the chef in there to cut it up into little pieces for me," he said like a mother would ask of their child's dinner. As the other three men laughed, I thought he was playing a joke on me and I stood there, perplexed. I assumed they'd begin to notice my bewilderment, but they still continued to joke. I eventually showed them to their seats and brought them their meals.

"Now Darlin', will you please stay and feed it to me?" he said chuckling with the other men. I was again baffled and just laughed along with them. Later, I asked Carolyn and Catriona about Dr. Spain's character. They explained that he was a doctor but he had had a stroke. "He comes in often with his friends," Catriona explained.

"Ya, but he is always making jokes as if he takes his condition ever so lightly," Carolyn said. I was beginning to see what it was like serving the food as opposed to eating it. As a waitress, you do just as the customer says and must be polite and respectable at all times, no matter what.

On Friday night, I waited on another regular, one who again struck me as very interesting. When he stepped into the restaurant I handed him and the man accompanying him menus and brought them drinks. As I mixed a glass of campari and orange, I studied him. Carolyn informed me that he was a very well known jeweler in town. Just as I had done with Mr. Spain, I also watched 'Matty the Jeweler' take the first sip of his drink. He slowly lifted the glass toward his extremely tanned and slightly wrinkled face and pouty lips, and with his lavishly jeweled pinky finger sticking straight up into the air, he took a small sip and set the glass back on the table. Every couple of minutes he would push a strand of his beautiful bleached blond hair out of his face and swing his head back dramatically. I enjoyed waiting on him that night because he was such a character. He too was a regular and Catriona noted that each time he came in he was with a different and younger man.

Later in the evening, Eugene checked on me to make sure things were going smoothly.

"I'm really getting the hang of this," I assured him. "I will definitely be ready for the wedding tomorrow."

By the night's end, I was exhausted and begged Paul to give me a ride home. If he hadn't, I would have slept in the restaurant.

When I arrived home, Aisling, Grainne, and Grainne's boyfriend Martin were in the bedroom watching a movie. Both of them had come home from school and had left their bags on the floor. The three of them sat in a line on the double bed staring at the T.V., devouring bags of popcorn, bars of chocolate, and cans of coke. Martin was a tall and skinny guy with longish, dark brown hair that fell just over his eyes and he was constantly brushing it out of his face. They happily greeted me and we reviewed our week apart from one another. I hopped onto the bed right next to Aisling and finished watching the movie with them, also finishing off the bags of popcorn and bars of chocolate. They both worked in the restaurant on weekends and I informed them that we had to be down there at ten thirty in the morning to help set up for the big wedding.

The next morning, we didn't leave the house till ten forty five and we rushed out of the house down the road to the restaurant. It was all commotion as trucks arrived with the centerpieces, consisting of pink, white, and yellow flowers. Bottles of our house red and white wine flowed in, as did fresh kegs and bottles of beer, and someone had also purchased two new bottles of vodka. The tables were aligned in a shape that allowed room for people to dance, but they were still bare and were to be covered with fresh, crisp white linen. On the floor near the bar sat three brooms, three mops and three buckets. There was also a note, which read:

Make those floor, and glasses shine so vibrantly that they could possibly blind somebody! I'll be back to check on you later.

-Eugene

The restaurant would be filled with close to one hundred people that night and we had our work cut out for us. The chef was frantically preparing plates of beef, chicken, and salmon as James and Eoghan helped prepare bowls of potatoes and vegetables. A beautifully crafted three-tier wedding cake had been delivered earlier that morning and was elegantly sitting in the refrigerator.

As I began to polish each glass in the restaurant one by one, Grainne and Aisling slaved over the floors, sweeping, mopping, and then waxing them. After we were done, we could see our reflections in every piece of crystal in the house and every inch of wood floor. Next we worked on the bathrooms, scrubbing toilets, shining mirrors and floors, and stocking up on toilet paper. Just as we had finished the bathrooms Eugene waltzed into the restaurant with his hand folded over his chest.

"Not bad, ladies. Not bad at all," he said. "Carolyn and Catriona are coming in at two o'clock and all the guests are arriving at four o'clock. You should probably start setting the tables now," he said, turning around to leave. A second later he peeked his head back in. "And make sure that silverware is polished!"

We didn't respond and I began to wipe down all the knives, forks, and spoons, as Aisling and Grainne put a tablecloth on every table. We set the tables in only an hour and thankfully had a little bit of time to relax before people arrived. Aisling and Grainne grabbed lunch and sat at the bar. I went across the street to the house to say hello to Biddy and Mary. The house was quiet. Mary had gone downtown with Bill and Eimear and Biddy had just woken up from her afternoon rest. She sat at the table eating some of her very own brown bread and drinking a cup of tea. I joined her at the table and gave her an overview of the work at Eugene's.

"There's a big wedding on today, so five of us are working. It's going to be crazy at the restaurant."

"I'd say it will be crazy," she replied.

"I love cake though so I'm definitely going to steal a piece," I told her jokingly.

"Well, actually," she said, 'there are lots of old myths about weddings.'

"Ooo, really?" I said in excitement because I knew she was about to tell me.

"You won't see this one tonight but in the old days, I remember seeing this at my auntie's wedding, the bride and groom each took three mouthfuls of salt and oatmeal to protect themselves against the power of the evil eye."

"Wow, that's strange! Where did they come up with that?" I asked. "It seems so phony, it's just not possible that it worked."

"Okay. Well, how about this one?" she began. "It is said that if a single woman puts a piece of wedding cake under her pillow when she sleeps, she will dream about her future husband."

"All right Biddy, I've had enough of your myths. I don't know about these notions!" I said getting up from the table. "I'm sorry but I'd better get back to work."

I laughed to myself on the way back to the restaurant. Biddy was always telling me about these different myths and stories. I wondered about their origins and what makes people believe in them. They couldn't be true. I just knew it.

Chapter 10

The wedding party, excluding the bride and groom, were the first guests to arrive. Four bridesmaids, the maid of honor, four groomsmen, the best man and the bride and groom's parents arrived around four fifteen, talking and laughing with large smiles on their faces. The five of us greeted them as they rushed to order drinks. People in groups began to rush through the doorway demanding drink and a good time. The music was loud enough to dance to, but quiet enough to talk over. So far about fifty people had arrived, and after the first round of drinks everyone loosened up and danced away. By five o'clock, the bride and the groom were in front of the restaurant. The guests stood silently surrounding the door as a man quietly played a song on the bagpipes. The couple entered and people began to cheer and shout and clap. The pile on the table that held all the presents grew larger and larger as more and more people arrived. I went into the kitchen to see how Aiden was doing. Well, let's just say it wasn't so good. He was rushing around the kitchen, lettuce flew through the air as he quickly made a couple of last minute salads, James was running around following Aiden's hysterical orders, and Eoghan was stirring the soup which was beginning to boil over. I was too afraid to ask if they needed help, so without them noticing, I slipped back out the door and into the bar.

At six, we urged everyone to find their seats so we could begin to serve dinner. At each table, depending on how many people it had, there were bottles of red and white wine and jugs of water along with a camera to randomly snap pictures. As soon as the salads were placed at each setting, people were in their seats. The bar was always crowded and the drinks were flowing. Clearly, everyone was having a good time.

"Vodka and tonic please!" a woman shouted.

"Three pints of Guinness and two glasses of Budweiser," a man demanded after her.

"Two more bottles of white at table three," Carolyn told me as she whisked past the bar back into the kitchen. After salad came the soup and then the main course.

"Since Paddy and Joe are staying in the pub, can I get their dinner?" one man asked me as I was serving. He had already finished his own.

"Can I have more spuds please?" two men at the other end of the table shouted just as I was heading into the kitchen.

Around seven o'clock, about half of the guests were considerably drunk and the lines to the bathrooms weren't getting any shorter. As people ate their meals, Grainne, Aisling, Carolyn, Catriona, and I had a chance to sit down and breathe for no more than ten minutes, before we had to fill more water jugs, make more drinks, bring out more potatoes and vegetables, make chips for the children, and start whipping cream for the cake. It was hectic and tiring.

"We better be getting one fat tip for this!" Catriona exclaimed before hopping out of her chair to go make chips. I laughed, but agreed and followed her into the kitchen to make whipped cream. I went to find Aiden, to ask where the cream was kept. I found him behind the kitchen having a cigarette break on an old stool and was sitting breathing heavily out of exhaustion. He didn't notice me standing near him.

"The worst is over now," I said getting his attention.

"Hah! Thank God!" he said. He wiped the sweat off his forehead with a cloth he pulled out of his pants' pocket.

"I just wanted to know where the cream is stored. We're going to serve the cake in about thirty minutes."

"All right, I'll be inside in a second to show you," he said taking a drag on his cigarette.

Finally, after all the plates were cleared and James and Eoghan had washed and dried the dishes, Aisling and I carried the

cake out into the restaurant and set it down on a table in front of the bride and groom. Suddenly everyone had their dancing shoes on and couples were jumping around the dance floor. I stood in front of the cake and whenever someone wanted a piece they danced on over. There were also pots of tea and coffee at each table for those who were not in the dancing mood. The newly married couple danced together slowly no matter the beat of the song, looking into each other's eyes as though it was the first time they had danced. Secretly I put five pieces of cake onto a plate and hid them behind the bar for us to enjoy as soon as the guests were distracted by the music. I took a bite into my piece and quickly spit it out.

"What the hell is this?" I asked the girls who were devouring their pieces. "Do you four have the same cake I do, because I'm having quite a different reaction to my first bite."

"It's wedding cake. I betcha the two mothers made it," Carolyn said.

"The icing is gorgeous," Grainne said.

I looked down at my piece. It was a heavy dark brown cake with raisins, currants, and other little pieces of fruit with thick white icing. It was neither soft nor fluffy and it tasted as though there was some alcohol in it. It was nothing like an American cake. I handed my piece off to Aisling who gladly took it.

It was only eight o'clock and the restaurant probably wouldn't be fully emptied until eleven, but at least our workload had slightly calmed down. The rest of the night consisted of drinks being poured and people having a good time. Various people at the wedding had brought instruments that they played and others sang songs. They played Irish folksongs for hours, and occasionally different people showed their talents or "party piece". It was 'ceol 'n craic' as the Irish say, which is music and good times. It was exciting to watch men and women get up to step dance as old men sang in their strong Irish brogues. The rest of the guests sat in their seats clapping their hands

and tapping their feet along with the beat of the bodhran and the fiddle.

Grainne, Aisling, Carolyn, Catriona, and I took turns washing and drying dishes while the others had a chance to sit down. During my turn I cut myself another piece of cake, wrapped it in foil and put it in my purse while nobody was watching. I didn't want the girls to see because they knew I didn't like the taste and would wonder why I was taking some home. Really, I don't know why I took a piece; I guess I just had a little more faith in myths by the end of the night.

By eleven thirty everyone was out the door. Some walked out, some stumbled out, and some were even carried out. By twelve, we were ready to go home and sleep. Unfortunately, Grainne, Aisling, and I were working in the morning for Sunday lunch. Thankfully though, I didn't have school on Monday for an Irish bank holiday so I would have plenty of time to rest before school on Tuesday. Or so I thought.

We made our way home and collapsed into bed. As soon as the light went out, so did Grainne and Aisling. I had one last thing to do. I leaned over and took the cake out of my purse, which was sitting on the floor and lightly placed it under my pillow. I felt even more ridiculous doing this when I felt the squish of the icing mush down under me, but I thought it was worth a try.

I woke the next morning in shock. I had had my recurring dream about the boy and the girl in the forest; only the boys face was perfectly clear this time. It was definitely the mystery boy. Biddy had told me I would dream about my future husband. I was pretty sure he wasn't my future husband, but my dream was close enough to the myth to be true! Grainne and Aisling were out of bed already so I could grab the flattened cake out from under my pillow and put it back in my purse until I had a chance to dump it in another bin.

Work was much easier because it was pouring down with rain and most people wanted to stay inside all day. Grainne, Aisling, and I had to walk to work mid-shower, but it was worth it to be drenched and have no customers. On our way home from work, the sun was beating down on us and people were out and about around Childers Park. And yet one more thankful event of my Sunday: tips! I had eighty euro in tips and one hundred and fifty euro for working five days straight. I was delighted with my accomplishment and myself. To my surprise, when we arrived home Jack informed me that Kiara had rung. I found her number on a piece of paper next to the phone in the hallway.

"Hello?" a woman's voice answered on the other end.

"Hi, may I speak to Kiara please?"

"One moment," said the woman.

"Hello?" a voice I recognized as Kiara's said.

"Hey, it's Sarah!"

"Oh, hey! I was just calling to tell you that Kate, Deirdre and I are going out tonight in Thurles, so you should come meet us!"

"I might, I'm wrecked from work but I might come down!" I said. "Call me from your mobile when you get to town and I'll see how I feel."

"All right. So maybe I'll see you later."

"Bye," I said hanging up the phone.

"What was that all about?," Aisling asked coming out of the room at the top of the stairs.

"Oh nothing," I said. "Some of the girls are going out tonight and they want me to meet them but I'm tired."

"What do you mean you're not going out?" she asked as though it was a ridiculous thought that I was tired and wanted to stay in. "Grainne and I will just have to drag you out then!"

"I don't know…" I began, but she cut me off.

"Nonsense, it will be great crack! Have a cup of coffee or something." I laughed at her effort and ability to persuade me, so I eventually agreed. For the next few hours we relaxed and recharged our batteries for the night. I was informed that a Monday bank holiday called for a fairly big Sunday night out because nobody works on a Monday bank holiday. I thought to myself, let's hope that includes all mysterious and handsome boys (wink! wink!). I decided it was time to tell Grainne and Aisling about the boy I might love. I first made them promise not to say a word to Jack, who still had his heart set on me marrying Declan. They were intrigued by my story and my deep interest in the boy.

"I think he's a friend of James because I saw them chatting the other night."

"What does he look like?" Grainne asked.

"We may know him!" Aisling added.

"I'm pretty sure he goes to the Christian Brothers with James and he's about the same height as him as well. He has short brown hair and the brightest blue eyes I've ever seen," I said beginning to daze off with a picture of him in my head.

"That doesn't really shorten the list," Aisling said. Most people in this town have brown hair and blue eyes."

"I guess we'll just have to wait and see tonight," Grainne said as she jumped off the bed and ran to the bathroom. "I call first shower!" While she was in the shower, Aisling and I decided what we were going to wear. Aisling chose a black skirt with black tights, a red long-sleeved V-neck top, and a pair of black boots. I, on the other hand, couldn't decide. I wanted to look hot, pretty, and casual - all at the same time. I wanted to catch his eye but not try too hard. Oh, the difficult job of picking out an outfit. I didn't have very many nicer looking, 'going out tops', but thankfully Grainne and Aisling had plenty. Grainne let me wear an emerald green loose top that showed the perfect amount of skin on my back. I paired it with a pair of

dark jeans and black pointy toe boots. Aisling went into the shower next, and while I waited, I wrote an e-mail to Sophie.

To: Polarbear99@aol.com

From: Sarbear15@hotmail.com

Hey girl,

Don't kill me but it's been almost two weeks since I wrote in the journal. A lot is going on with me! Okay well, my friends Kiara, Kate, Deirdre, and I are going to Dublin (Ireland's capital and largest city) in two weeks to shop. We're going to stay with Kiara's aunt there and the girls may even show me a couple of different things around the city. We're taking the train and everything. It's going to be great! At first there was a problem though. I didn't have any money for the train or to shop so now I have a job waitressing in the restaurant my uncle owns. It's a lot of fun and some ridiculous characters come in to dine. I'm going out with my cousins and my friends tonight and I hope to see the boy I was telling you about. Hopefully I'll actually get to talk to him! I really miss you and I wish you were here!

Lots of love. Your busy friend, Sarah

Finally it was my turn to take a shower. I went in and started scrubbing my hair and body. After working all day yesterday and today, the hot water felt great.

"EEEkkkk!" I screamed nearly falling out of the shower and pulling the curtain down with me. Grainne and Aisling came running toward the bathroom door.

"What, what?" Grainne screamed though the door.

"Are you all right?" Aisling said.

"Yes, I'm fine! Just the two of you hogged all the hot water and now I'm freezing!" I screamed back. I heard them laughing from inside the bathroom. I finished up quickly so I wouldn't freeze to death. I walked into the bedroom where

Grainne stood naked rubbing fake tan all over her legs and Aisling had her hair flipped over for the blow-dryer. They looked up at me and smiled innocently. Grainne wasn't nearly as open with me when I first arrived but the three of us had grown to a certain comfort level with one another. It was especially nice because I felt like they were my sisters; they certainly acted like my sisters.

"Oh shut up!" I said to them going to sit down next to the heater before I dressed. They laughed again but kept on doing their own thing. "What time do you think we're going to leave to go out tonight?" I called over the roar of the blow dryer.

"I'd say we'll head out around seven," she hollered back at me. I looked over to the little clock that sat on the stand next to my bed. It said ten after five. Since I had plenty of time and my stomach was growling, I threw on a bathrobe and went downstairs to eat. Jack and Una both were in the kitchen. Una was sitting on the couch watching T.V. and Jack was making a cup of tea.

"Hello dear!" Una shouted. "I haven't seen you in ages. How's working in the restaurant?"

"It's great. I like it a lot."

"Are you wrecked, pet?" she asked.

"No, I'm fine. So far anyway," I assured her. I opened the fridge and grabbed a variety of things, a yogurt, a bag of ham, a block of cheese, and a jar of mayonnaise. I grabbed a knife, a spoon, two slices of bread, and a bag of crisps. I made a sandwich and headed into the sitting room to watch television as I ate. Jack followed after me.

"So, how are things with Declan?" he of course asked.

"Fine," I said lying.

"That's good. Be careful not to overwork yourself," he said, thankfully changing the subject.

"I won't," I told him, hoping to end the conversation. I wasn't in the mood to chat. I wanted to sit and enjoy my sandwich with his silent company.

At ten after seven, the three of us walked down the road toward the pub. People stood outside smoking and chatting with their beer in hand, and inside the doorway stood crowds of pcople. I followed Aisling and Grainne through the crowd as we made our way to the far corner of the bar to our 'gang'. There were some people who I recognized from previous nights out and some who I didn't know at all. They were all happily drinking and chatting. I whispered in Grainne's ear that I was going to the bathroom. As I weaved through the crowds of people, I searched though my purse for my lip-gloss. Carelessly, my head was down and I walked straight into someone who had just come out of the men's bathroom. I looked up, about to apologize. Standing right in front of me, looking at me, smiling at me, it was him. I stood there silent, a victim of panic and disorientation, hoping he would say something. Silence. We just looked at each other and at the same time we stuck out our hands and began to introduce ourselves.

"Hi, I'm Sar-"

"Hi, I'm Liam."

"Hi," I said, not knowing what to say next.

"It's nice to finally meet you," he said laughing. We were reading each other's minds. We had seen each other, we had noticed each other, but we had never spoken. I was blushing now and was staring at the floor fiddling with the lip-gloss that was still in my hand. He grabbed my hand and my attention. "Can I buy you a drink?" I went to sit down at a small table in the corner where there were two vacant stools. I made eye contact with Grainne from across the room and pointed at Liam. She gave me a big smile and a thumb up.

"Your cousin is James, right?" Liam asked sitting down across from me.

"Yea," I said. "Do you know him?"

"We go to school together."

We went over the basics, age, school, siblings etc. James had already told him a little about me because, to my surprise, Liam had asked. Liam had lots of questions about America, where I was from, what it was like to live there, and how it was different from Thurles. Neither of us could stop smiling, it was actually quite humorous. After a while James walked by, he was heading to the bathroom.

"Hey you. You better be nice to my cousin or I'll bust ya," James said to Liam half jokingly but a little serious. I laughed but gave him a look that told him to be on his way. Up close Liam was just as good looking as he was from a distance. He had about as much facial hair as any seventeen-year-old male might get, and when he laughed I noticed he had the cutest little dimples. He was shy but mysterious and I liked that about him. As friends of his passed by he was a complete gentleman and introduced me. In a bit, I glanced towards the pub door as Declan entered. I made a face, which Liam quickly noticed.

"What's the matter?" he asked. "Is that your boyfriend or something?" he added and I could tell he secretly hoped it wasn't my boyfriend. I stood up from the table and grabbed Liam's hand, pulling him up with me.

"Far from it," I said, dragging him with me. "Can we go outside for a minute? I need some fresh air." I walked a little ways down the sidewalk away from people who were outside surrounded by clouds of smoke and sat down on a ledge in front of a shop. He followed and sat down with me.

"Sorry about that," I said. "It's just that guy, Declan, he likes me and my Uncle tries to set us up because my Uncle likes him, but I don't want to meet Declan."

"Oh right," he said. "Why would your Uncle make you go out with someone?"

"Well my Uncle is his hurling coach, and has looked out for him since Declan was young. He's almost like a son to him. It really unfair but I'm living with Jack and am sometimes forced to see Declan." Just as we were getting back into

conversation Kiara, Kate, and Deirdre walked past without noticing me.

"Hey ladies!" I shouted. They slowly turned around.

"Oh hey!" they all shouted back, realizing it was me.

"I didn't even see you sitting there," Kate said. "I'm glad you decided to come out."

"This is Liam. Liam, this is Kate, Kiara, and Deirdre," I said giving the girls a look to hint that he was the one I had been telling them about. They stood silent for a minute and then finally understood.

"Oh, um, Liam! Right. Hi Liam," Kiara said.

"I'll be back inside in a minute guys," I said hoping they would understand and go into the pub. "Oh by the way Declan's in there Kate," I said giving her a wink. "And Kiara, James is in there as well, and Deirdre, he's got a couple cute friends." The three of them smiled excitedly and headed toward the door. I laughed and explained to Liam that Kate liked Declan and Kiara liked James.

"Well, then who's left for you to like?" he said smiling slightly. I started blushing again and stared at the ground. He laughed lightly, and so did I. He gently lifted my chin with his hand and looked into my eyes. He moved closer to my face and as my eyes were naturally closing because he was obviously about to kiss me, I saw Declan leave the pub and see me. He looked shocked and extremely let down. My eyes opened wide as he walked toward us. I feared what he might say to Liam and me. I coughed so Liam would know to stop and he turned around to see Declan's angry face. Declan appeared to be drunk by the way he was stumbling toward us. He lifted his hand to punch Liam and completely missed, hitting the wall and hurting himself.

"Declan, just go home. You really should leave," I said looking away from him in shame. Kate ran out of the pub after him and of course offered to walk him home. I let her only because he wouldn't make it himself.

"I am so sorry Liam. I've never seen him like that."

"Don't worry about it," he said putting his hand on my shoulder to comfort me. It was close to twelve now and people were pouring out of the pub to go to the nightclub. Grainne and her boyfriend came out followed by Paul and Aisling, James, Kiara, and Deirdre, and some random guy I didn't recognize. I guess Kiara caught James' eye and one of his friends noticed Deirdre. Aisling called to me to come along. Liam put his arm around me and we walked to the nightclub together. He immediately whisked me onto the dance floor. The way he held me and looked at me made me melt inside. He was so sweet and I hoped I would see him again. We danced for hours as if we were the only two people in the room. It felt amazing. He leaned in to whisper something into my ear.

"I have a confession to make," he began. "I know I only met you tonight, but-" before he could finish Kate appeared back from out of nowhere.

"Sarah, I need you. Deirdre left. She's outside," she said to me in a deep panic. "She must have eaten or drunk something bad that made her sick. I don't know. Just we have to go." I had to leave no matter how badly I wanted to stay.

"When am I going to see you?" he asked with concern in his eyes.

"After school on Tuesday. I'll meet you in the square!" I said as our hands slowly tore apart. I had to run off with Kate to find Kiara and pull her away from James. I looked back one last time. Liam stood there in the middle of the crowd of chaotic dancers, watching me as if he couldn't take his eyes off me and if he did, even for one second, he would never see me again. I disappeared through the doorway and out of his sight.

Chapter 11

When I woke up Monday morning, I lay in bed for a long time just staring at the sky and remembering the previous night. Aisling and Grainne were still passed out in the bed next to me; they had arrived home much later than me. Moments later, Grainne pried open one eye and noticed me smiling from ear to ear.

"Hmm, I wonder why you're smiling?" she said sarcastically. I turned, looked at her, and continued smiling.

"He's lovely, Sarah," Aisling added still face down with her head ensconced between two pillows.

"I know!"

"Are you going to meet him?" Grainne asked.

"Well, I want to but I don't know what to do about Declan. I feel so horrible and I don't want to hurt him, not to mention that I would have to hide it from Jack. He's in love with the chap," I said, surprised at how Irish I had just sounded. I certainly had to figure something out if I wanted to keep seeing Liam.

"I don't think you not dating Declan is actually the problem," Grainne said.

"What do you mean?" I asked, confused. Aisling turned over onto her side, her eyes partially opened, ready to engage a bit more in conversation.

"About twenty years ago Daddy was in a business. His good friend Jim and him owned a pub. Business was great and they did real well. After a couple years they started feuding a bit over the money. When business wasn't so good they each thought the other was at fault."

"It was all downhill from there," Aisling continued. "The two of them disagreed on how the pub should have been run, and were in constant argument over who had more ownership of the pub. Soon enough Jim was fed up, cheated Daddy out of loads of money, and moved on."

"That's terrible," I said.

"Daddy lost loads of money, and the pub," Grainne added.

"I don't quite understand one thing though."

"What?" Grainne said.

"What does this have to do with my Liam/Declan situation?"

"Oh right. I almost forgot," Aisling said. "Jim is Liam's father."

I gasped. My heart started pounding and my palms began to sweat.

"Daddy's a bit bitter about the whole thing. I'd say your best bet is to keep quiet about it." Grainne suggested.

"Jack's been so nice to me. I just wouldn't feel right lying to his face like that. I'll talk to him," I said falling backwards and letting my head hit the pillow hard. I grabbed a second pillow, covered my face, and screamed into it as loud as I could. Why me? Why this guy? Why couldn't Jack hate Declan's father? Thoughts raced through my head as I decided what my next move would be.

I leaned over to see the time, eleven thirty. I hopped out of bed with a plan.

"I have to talk to Declan," I said aloud, once out of bed. I grabbed the brush off the dresser, fixed my hair up into a ponytail, put on a pair of jeans and a t-shirt. I went into the bathroom and washed my face and brushed my teeth. When I came back into the bedroom Grainne and Aisling had both

dozed off again. I put on the first pair of shoes I saw lying on the floor, grabbed a sweatshirt, went downstairs without saying a word to Jack or Una, and slammed the door behind me. Just as I had suspected, Declan was sitting on the wall in front of his house with two of his friends. It was a nice day and the glare from the sun kept me from seeing the other two boys' faces. I walked toward him determined to tell him exactly how I felt about his behavior. He saw me walking toward him and said something to his friends. They turned and saw me coming and walked off in the opposite direction.

"Look, don't say anything. Just let me explain myself," he said before I had even reached him. When I finally stood before him, I noticed things about his looks and his actions that I had never seen before. I was so ashamed of the previous night when I had seen things in him I never wanted to see. His face wasn't calm or comforting, as it had been when I first met him. I looked inside him and felt confused.

"Listen. I like you. I like you a lot. I was jealous and I shouldn't have done what I did but I'm not going to deny how it made me feel, and pretty much, it felt bad, but I understand your disappointment in me."

"Well, I am disappointed in you. Basically it was so out of character and I feel like I don't even know you anymore." I was frustrated just looking at him and I turned to leave. He grabbed my hand and jumped off the wall. He swung me around toward him and kissed my lips hard. He squeezed my arms like he was never letting me go. When we separated I looked at him with disgust. He searched my face for hope, a little spark inside me that I knew wasn't there. Deep down he knew it too. I slapped his face just as hard as he had kissed me and walked away without looking back to see the shocked look on his face. When I came back inside, Jack was standing in the hallway.

"Whatever he did to make you that mad was a mistake. Just give him another chance," he said. "He's a good kid; a nice kid." He walked away into the kitchen with his cup of tea in hand and I realized that it was in fact a demand. I followed him right into the kitchen and sat down in the chair directly across from him.

"I need to talk to you," I said staring him in the face. "I don't like Declan any more than a friend. I like this boy Liam-" Before I could say another word his hand was up in the air directing me to stop speaking.

"I know exactly who you're talking about and I forbid you to see him. He is a liar, a cheater, and I don't approve," he said returning to his tea and scone. "Look, I know Declan. He's like a son to me and I know you'll like him too."

"Just because you had problems with Liam's father doesn't mean he's the same," I said to plead my case.

"Like father, like son, my dear. And I won't say another word about it." I stood up from my chair, red faced, went into the sitting room and got straight into my e-mail. I desperately needed to vent.

To: `Polarbear99@aol.com`

From: `Sarbear15@hotmail.com`

Sophie-

Drama, Drama, Drama. That's all I can say to sum up my life right now. There's good news, bad news, and very confusing news. First I'll go with the good news. I finally met the mystery boy, who by the way I think is the love of my life. His name is Liam and he's absolutely gorgeous from every angle. Last night I ran into him (literally)

when I was walking to the bathroom in a pub. We talked and danced the whole night, and he's basically perfect: It's a little too good to be true. Ah! And that it is. Here comes the bad news. Declan (the guy who likes me but I don't like and my Uncle basically forces on me) was there, and not very excited to see Liam and I together. As for the confusing news. Turns out that Liam is the son of a man named Jim, who my Uncle Jack once did business with. Unfortunately, business ended badly and Jack hates Liam's father, therefore, he hates Liam. I don't know what to do but I know that I'm not letting Liam go. That's for sure! However, in the midst of the unfortunate aspects of my life at the moment, Liam makes me forget my troubles. I know I'm turning into a total sap over here but I can't help it. I'm meeting him tomorrow after school and I can hardly wait till then!

Your lovesick friend, Sarah

The day continued as if it was in slow motion but I went to bed early because I was eagerly and impatiently awaiting Tuesday's arrival.

Since I had gone to bed so early, I also woke up early. I had time to have a leisurely breakfast and a considerably long shower. I put on a little make-up and wore an enormous smile on my face. I arrived early at the bank to meet the girls, but I was glad to wait outside. The morning sun was warming the town as it rose over the chimneys and it felt good as it shone on my face. When they came off the bus, all four of us had news of our new and hopeful relationships and all sorts of gossip from our exciting night out.

"I really think I'm getting somewhere with him. He's going to come around, don't you think?" Kate asked us, referring to

Declan. Advice is what you ask for when you already know the answer but wished you didn't, so I decided to tell her what she wanted to hear.

"I'm sure he will." However, I knew there was no relationship developing between them. I didn't want her to be bitter at me for suggesting she give up trying. Thankfully, she missed the part where Declan tried to punch Liam out of jealousy for me. Declan had behaved like an ass. I wondered what Kate could possibly see in him?

"So what about you, Deirdre? Who was the cute lad you were chatting with?" Kate asked.

"His name's Tommy. I didn't get to talk to him for too long because I told him I was starting to feel sick and I had to go. I gave him my mobile number and he sent me a text yesterday to see how I was feeling.

"That's really sweet!" I said.

"Okay so anyways," Kiara said as she began to ramble off, "James and I didn't talk that much either."

"Oh, that's okay. You can talk to him more the next time we're out," Deridre said, reassuring her.

"Oh, no, no. I think you misunderstood me. We weren't talking because our mouths were busy," she said, giving us each a wink and a giant smile. The three of us looked at her and laughed.

"Okay. So I'm meeting Liam after school," I said, preparing to tell them my story. I couldn't exactly explain that I had a slight dilemma because Kate would be furious. "But honestly guys, I think I've fallen in love!" I said, shocked at myself for feeling that way. The four of us walked happily in a line the rest of the way to school, each of us with a smile on her face and a certain handsome someone on her mind.

"At least we have Celtic Mythology today. It's the least boring class and that will make the day go by faster," I told them, hoping that it would in fact go by faster than usual. "The faster it goes, the sooner I see him again!"

Before class started, everyone caught up on the events of their long weekend. Miss Dwyer entered the classroom and we partook in our usual morning ritual. We stood for her and recited the *Hail Mary* and the *Our Father* then sat down and prepared to hear stories and learn of new and exotic creatures. Instead, she told us some very exciting news.

"Our class will be taking a camping trip," she began animatedly. Everyone looked around, confused but intrigued. "We will be spending one night sleeping amongst the stars at the Devil's Bit." We then looked around wanting to hear more. "We will hike, tell stories, and maybe even conjure up some of the ideas I have introduced to you to during class these last few months."

"This is going to be so much fun!" I said, not realizing the teacher was still talking and I had shouted out to the class. Miss Dwyer laughed.

"Agreed, Sarah," she said, delighted to see someone else feeling the same way. "The Devil's Bit, as many of you may know, is an enchanted place, and we will embrace the mythological scenery within the forest. I organized this for your class only because I think you deserve something extra related to Celtic Mythology. Also, I think we should show Sarah a little something outside our town," she said, smiling at me.

"Wow, thank you so much. I'm really looking forward to it!" I told her. "When are we going?"

"In May. The weather will be a bit nicer, which will enable us to truly enjoy our surroundings," she said, speaking as if, in her mind, she was already there.

We spent the rest of the time discussing the history of the Devil's Bit and Miss Dwyer explained the "agenda for our adventure," as she put it.

I left the school at the end of the day with permission slips to bring home to Jack and Una and a vast smile on my face. First, I was going to see Liam, and in addition to that I was eager for my trip to Dublin in two weeks, and now the trip to the Devil's Bit, which sounded as though it was going to be amazing. As I left the building, alone, without any of the other girls, I had two unusual feelings. And I became worried. What if Liam didn't meet me? What if he had already forgotten about me? I feared the embarrassment and the pain I would suffer. Then, on the other hand, I had butterflies flipping every which direction inside me. If he did show up, which I hoped and prayed that he would, I didn't know what I would say to him. I was nervous and excited at the same time. I walked past the many shoe shops, past the post office and up toward the bank where I met the girls each morning and there stood Liam. He leaned against the wall, chatting with his friends and laughing extremely hard revealing his teeth. In his fit of laughter he looked toward me and noticed me approaching him. He ran toward me with a glorious smile on his face. He kissed my forehead as if he had been doing it for years, as if it was nothing, and he was comfortable enough with me to do so in front of his friends. It warmed my insides and I felt safe, allowing my butterflies to disappear completely. In just a day I had forgotten how he made me feel and how at ease I felt around him. One look into his eyes, and that was all the assurance I needed. He made me act completely natural, and when we were together I didn't have a care in the world, and it felt good.

We held hands as we walked back toward my school. We crossed the street and headed toward a small path that went along the river.

"I couldn't stop thinking about you yesterday," I said, shocked at myself for revealing such intimate information.

"I know. Me too," he said returning the favor. "I feel like I've known you for years," he said quietly. It was sweet how he became slightly embarrassed when he was saying something nice to me. We walked silently, enjoying each other's company. We eventually reached a nice spot by the river with a tree and a patch of grass. We sat next to each other, leaning against the tree's trunk.

"So Liam. I still don't even know your last name," I said almost not believing it myself. How did I feel so much for someone I hardly knew? It was beginning to freak me out.

"Carroll. Liam Carroll," he said, laughing.

"So who are you anyway? What do you like to do? What's your family like?"

"I'm assuming Aisling and Grainne informed you of our conflict at hand?" he asked.

"Yea, they did," I said looking to the ground. I couldn't even look him in the eyes.

"I don't care. So you shouldn't either," he said. I looked up feeling completely reassured and smiled.

"I don't care at all," I assured him. "But my Uncle does."

"Don't worry about it," he said putting his hands on my face. They were warm and soft and comforting.

"Okay," I responded.

"Anyways, on a happier note. Where do I begin? I, along with my three older brothers, play Rugby. My father played Rugby, as did all his brothers. I have one sister. She's seven. My mother died just after my sister was born, so my aunt took care of us for a while when we were young. I want to go to college

after school and I want to be a doctor, but don't tell anyone that part. Nobody else knows."

I put my hand on his shoulder. "I'm so sorry about your mother. I had no idea."

"Don't," he began. "I've spent my whole life grieving. It's mostly hard seeing my dad. He'll never get over it." He started looking upset and I quickly changed the subject.

"Okay, now my turn!" I said putting my voice and mood back into a higher and more enthusiastic pitch. "My father is a carpenter and my mother is a teacher," I began. "I've one sister, Morgan, but she's already in college. I don't play any sports. I love to write but still, I have no idea what I want to do when I go to college. Pretty much I don't have my life quite as figured out as you have. I'm happy to be here. I was bored at home, kind of lost I guess. It sounds stupid I'm sure, but I just felt I needed to leave. I needed a break to search for the real me. It's very cliché, but something was missing from my life in Syracuse."

"Have you found it here in Thurles?" he asked.

"I think I just might have," I said smiling at him shyly, and blushing. He too was smiling.

Chapter 12

Liam and I agreed to meet after school on Wednesday and he planned on walking me to work. Time was flying by now and I wanted to leave Ireland with no regrets and as many memories as my mind could hold. I dreaded Friday night when I again had to go to the movies with Declan. I refrained from telling Liam about it because I didn't want him to get jealous or upset with me. I truly liked Declan as a friend and as a friend only, but so long as he did not stop liking me as more than a friend, and so long as Jack supported Declan's quest, I had to go out with him, however much against my will.

I kissed Liam's cheek at the front of the shop before I went inside to go to work and he walked back to town to catch the next bus.

"I'll see you tomorrow after school," he said as he walked away down the street. I smiled and blew him a kiss.

Aiden was already at work in the kitchen, chopping up vegetables and pre-making bowls of salad.

"Hey Aiden! How are you?" I said practically floating through the kitchen.

"Someone's in a good mood," he said, noticing that I was on cloud nine.

"Right you are." I said making my way through the swinging door and into the restaurant. I had arrived before Carolyn and Catriona and began to set the tables. I turned the music to an upbeat station and danced around as I set the tables, singing into the spoons like they were microphones. I was so utterly caught up in my stimulating work ethic that I didn't even

notice the two girls enter the restaurant. They were now standing at the bar watching me and laughing hysterically.

"Nice show, sweetie!" Carolyn said after she turned the music down.

"Bravo!" Catriona added.

"Oh, I didn't even notice you come in," I said laughing at myself in a bit of awkwardness. "Anyway," I began, hoping we could pretend they had missed all that, "I already set the tables. We just have to clean the floors and the bathrooms." They stood there for a couple of minutes more just staring at me and we all eventually went our separate ways to get back to work.

As soon as I unlocked the door at six o'clock sharp, Mary, Bill, Eimear, Nora and her mom arrived to sit down and have a quick bite to eat. Since no one else was in the restaurant yet, I sat down with them to chat for a few minutes.

"How is everything? Do you like working in the restaurant?" Mary asked me.

"Hi! Sarah," Eimear said tugging on my arm to catch my attention. "Can I please have a fizzy orange?"

"Sure, you can sweetie." By the time I came back with her drink they were all ready to order. They didn't stay much later than seven, leaving right around the time when four women came in together. Catriona waited on them but I observed the women as they drank their bottle of white wine and discussed their lives. From the way they were dressed and took care of themselves, it appeared that they had money. They talked about their husbands quite a bit. When I helped Catriona serve them their main courses they had complaints and changes. They were the kind of customers we liked to call "high maintenance". Our work was cut out for us, running in and out of the kitchen, waiting on them hand and foot. Not many more

customers came in during the night. Since it was so quiet, we were able to close at nine-thirty instead of ten. I decided to grab a snack from the shop and go up to the house for a bit. Joe was upstairs helping Bill get ready for bed and Eimear, Mary, and Biddy sat in the sitting room. Paul wasn't around and I suspected he was with James and Eoghan somewhere. There wasn't much on television, which gave us a chance to talk more.

"I met a boy. He's lovely."

"Oh, did ya! What's his name?" Mary said as though she was happy for me.

"Liam Carroll," I told the two of them.

"Oh," Mary and Biddy said solemnly at the same time.

"I'm sure Jack has an earful to say about you seeing Liam Carroll," Mary said.

"He doesn't approve but I'm not letting that stop me," I said, hoping they wouldn't disapprove of me going against Jack's will.

"Good girl," Biddy said. "Those are nice looking fellows, the Carrolls."

"I think so too," I agreed. "He's very nice and I'm feeling happy," I said, picturing Liam's face in my mind. "I can't tell Jack though. He's still stuck on me meeting that lad, Declan."

"Don't mind Jack," Biddy said. "The man's been off his knob since he was born," she said laughing. Mary and I laughed along with her.

"Jack is so nice to me and I love living with him. I almost feel like I owe him something. Aw! well! It'll work out eventually," I said, feeling incredibly hopeful.

Paul eventually came in and I persuaded him to give me a lift home around ten-thirty.

I went to say goodnight to Jack and Una when I arrived home. Una was already up in bed and Jack was, of course, in his usual spot in the sitting room. I sat down on the couch next to him without saying anything. He turned to me and began to tell me a story about my father as a boy.

"When we were kids we would have to herd up the cattle every morning before we had to head off to school," he began. It was extremely random, but at least he was starting a conversation with me that didn't involve Declan in it.

"Really?" I replied, acting interested.

"Your father used to hate doing it to. He thought it was such an annoyance. He put up such a fight," he said chuckling to himself, his round stomach popping up and down. I smiled because he looked cute as he remembered my father as a child. It felt nice to be talking to him.

"Declan came by to see you tonight," he said. "I reminded him you were working."

"Oh, okay, thanks," I responded. I suddenly wasn't in the mood to sit and talk to Jack after he had reminded me of my situation with Declan. "Goodnight," I said, walking out of the room and upstairs to bed.

On Thursday at four o'clock, I stood outside the shop before heading into work, watching Liam walk back toward the square. I hoped Eugene was in his office because I needed to ask permission to be off work on Friday.

"Hey, is Eugene in the office?" I asked the girl standing behind the counter.

"I don't know. I've only just begun my shift," she replied as she began restacking bars of chocolate into the enormous selection placed at the front of the shop. I tapped lightly on the office door.

"Come in," Eugene said. I entered the office to see him hunched over his desk counting money, carefully placing each bill in its proper pile. I saw the steam rising from the fresh cup of tea set by his side. He didn't even look up to see who had come in.

"Eugene, its Sarah."

"Well Sarah? How are you? Are you handling work all right?" he asked, sounding concerned and taking his attention away from the money. "I noticed you doing an okay job in there the other night."

"Oh. It's great. I really enjoy it."

"So will you be working for the rest of your stay here?" he asked, as if it was assumed that I would be.

"Really? That would be excellent."

"But…" he said already knowing that there was one coming.

"I have to ask you a favor..." I began.

"I don't do favors. Just business," he told me, going back to his money.

"I was wondering if it would be all right if I took this Friday night off," I asked, nervous for his response. Even to me it seemed like such a preposterous proposal, since I had just been hired.

"That's fine," he replied simply. "Now get in there and get to work," he demanded. I scurried out of the office lest he change

his mind, and decided I would ask him about the night I needed off to go to Dublin another time.

Unlike most days, I wished Friday had gone by extremely slow. I dreaded my date with Declan, but since I didn't have to work, I had time to see Liam after school. We agreed to meet at the place by the river where we'd been two days before. When I arrived Liam was already waiting for me. I lay down next to where he was sitting and rested my head in his lap. He lightly brushed the hair off my face and smiled down at me.

"It's good to see you," he said.

"Same to you," I replied.

"Why didn't you have to work tonight?" he asked out of curiosity. I couldn't really tell him why I wasn't working, but I hesitated lying to him. I had no other choice.

"He just gave me the night off. I guess he sensed I needed a little break," I said, already feeling completely guilty.

"Well I wish I could see you tonight, but I've got a Rugby match." I was thankful he didn't ask to see me because I would have to quickly think up another lie. "Anything new and exciting in your life?"

"Yes, actually. I completely forgot to tell you this on Tuesday. My class is taking a camping trip to the Devil's Bit in a month. Isn't that great? We've been learning about Celtic Mythology and all that."

"Oh, really? That's interesting. Maybe I'll just have to sneak up there and meet you in the middle of the night," he suggested mysteriously. "It's actually quite near my house. I've climbed to the top loads of times. So, what are you planning on doing at the Devil's Bit?"

"We're going to hike, tell stories, and possibly re-live myths of the enchanted and magical place as my teacher referred to it."

"Sounds good," he laughed. For a while we sat silently, listening to the sound of the water slowly drift by and the occasional wind that rustled the leaves and sent chills through my body. We both lost track of time and suddenly had to hurry in separate directions. Liam had to go and meet his team to prepare for his match, and I had to get home to meet Declan. Sadly, we wouldn't be able to see each other again until Monday.

"Good luck in your match," I said as he hugged me goodbye.

"I'll miss you this weekend," he replied kissing me on the cheek and rushing off. I watched him jog away and then quickly headed home myself.

I pulled my hair out of the ponytail it had been in for the last hour, ran a brush through it, and dabbed a bit of lip-gloss on my lips. I wore a pair of loose and comfortable jeans and a plain white long sleeved shirt so I wouldn't be cold in the movie theater. I grabbed ten euro from the top drawer of the night stand next to my bed, told Jack I was leaving and walked toward Declan's house. I was a few minutes early but I didn't want him to formally pick me up from my house. I lifted my fist to knock on the door and it opened. Declan appeared in the doorway in front of me. He didn't grace me with his usual smile or gentlemenly manners.

"Let's go," he said, shutting the door behind him and walking past me. I was confused, but followed him out of the gate and down the road. He was walking extremely fast and I was almost running to keep up with him.

"Wait up. What's the rush?" I practically shouted at him. He stopped short and waited for me to come into view next to him before he started walking again. I grabbed his arm, forcing him to stop. "What is wrong with you?" He shook his head and stared at me for a minute before answering.

"Sorry. I just had something on my mind. That's all. I'm fine now," he assured me before turning to continue walking. Thankfully, he slowed his pace down considerably and acted as if I was actually there with him.

"How did your week at school go?" I asked, trying to make conversation.

"It was all right, I suppose," he replied. "How was yours?"

"Great!" I said enthusiastically. "My class and I are going on a camping trip to the Devil's Bit for a night in May."

"For what?" he asked, essentially seeming interested.

"Hike, tell stories, enjoy the stars. I'm not sure really," I replied. I wasn't in the mood to explain the whole Celtic Mythology story. By then we had reached the theater. I was starving because I had missed dinner. He transformed back into gentlemen mode, paying for my ticket, popcorn, diet coke, and bar of chocolate, and I didn't complain. I liked this Declan better, the real Declan, and the one I had become such good friends with when I first arrived. We sat silently as the theater began to fill up and we waited for *Man on Fire* to begin. It was gruesome but entertaining, and by the end we both agreed it was good. We stood up from our seats, and I brushed popcorn crumbs off my pants. He lightly touched my hand. I looked up and he leaned in to kiss me. Since he had caught me off guard, he succeeded and landed his lips right on top of mine. He held my cheeks roughly, hoping to persuade me to return the kiss. As I pushed him off me, I noticed two

girls who had stood up from their seats just across the aisle from us. I looked closer through the dimness of the theater to see Kate and Amy staring right at Declan and I. Their jaws were practically touching the horrible maroon carpeting on the theater floor. The look on Kate's face let me know that she was hurt and disillusioned. The two of them ran swiftly out of the theater and I noticed tears rushing down Kate's face. I pushed Declan out of the way and chased after them. I caught Kate's shoulder outside the cinema. "It's not what you think!" I told her, hoping she would let me explain.

"Yea, I'm sure," she replied sarcastically while still crying hysterically. Now people who were leaving the theater were staring at us.

"I don't know what to say, Kate. If you'd please just let me explain," I pleaded.

"Don't say anything, Sarah. You just aren't the friend I thought I'd made," she said, scolding me right where it hurt. Amy rushed over and pulled her away from me, the two of them disappearing down the street. I stood there desperate and sad, not knowing what to do next. I needed to give her time to cool off and hoped she would eventually let me explain. Before I knew it, she would have all the girls hating me and the rest of the school year would be miserable. I turned around to see Declan standing there waiting for the "episode" to be over so we could continue our date. Little did he know he had caused this all to happen. In my mind I pictured myself jumping on top of him and beating him to a pulp. I glanced back at him and ran away from the cinema toward home. I hoped he would get the hint and not run after me. Fortunately he did.

I felt so horrible that Kate had seen us and at the worst moment. Why did he have to keep trying to make things work

between us? I turned to the only person who would understand. I needed to vent my feelings to someone, something, or anything. I headed straight to the computer.

ꕤ

To: `Polarbear99@aol.com`

From: `Sarbear15@hotmail.com`

Sophie,

It never ends. I am in a lover's quarrel.

Tonight I had a date with Declan. We went to the movies. Everything was comfortable and I wasn't feeling awkward and he had to go and ruin everything. At the end of the movie he kissed me, and the worst part is, my friend Kate, who likes him, was also at the movies and saw it happen. I didn't even know she was there until I saw her standing, staring at me in shock as though I had just betrayed her. Everything is so mixed up. She likes Declan. Declan likes me. I like Liam. Oh Liam! Even his name makes everything better. (I'm smiling right now, by the way.) Hee! hee! Anyways I just feel horrible because Kate had the completely wrong impression and I don't know what to do. If only you were here. I know you would make everything better. Miss you bunches (especially right now).

Love, your confused friend, Sarah

ꕤ

I had a head full of bewildering and stressful thoughts that kept me from falling asleep. I wished there was something or someone who could make everything right. I wished some greater force would swoop through and make everything better. I greatly feared the consequences of Kate's anger and everyone else's reaction at school Monday. I eventually fell asleep and had great dreams about happier and much less baffling times.

The next morning I was in a desperate need to clear my head. I decided to visit Biddy because she always cheered me up and found solutions to my problems. The yard was filled with many people I didn't recognize, mostly little girls, who were tending to the horses. Mary was in the arena with Eimear and Nora directing seven children who were trotting atop seven horses in a circle.

Biddy sat in a tall stool chair in front of the stove, cooking the dinner and watching out the window into the yard.

"Well, Sarah? Are you staying for dinner? Go down to the shop and get yourself a cut of steak for me to cook for you," she insisted. Before I could ask for her guidance I had to eat. If I refused dinner she would find a way to force me to eat. It was a great trait about her, because I was in fact hungry. When I came back up she hadn't moved from her seat and sat watching the potatoes boil and the steak grill.

"What should I do?" I asked her after explaining my dilemma.

"Ah, I think everything will work out somehow. You just wait and see. 'The course of love never did run smooth'," she said giving me a wink and returning her focus back toward the steak.

"What do you mean? That doesn't make sense to me," I said, just as puzzled as when we had begun the conversation.

"Don't worry about it dear. It'll be fine," she said as if she was absolutely positive. She was sure of her conclusions, however, I was not so sure. How were things supposed to just work out? Her words had confused me even more, and filled me with doubt.

Chapter 13

Oh, what a tangled web we weave, when first we practice to deceive.

-Sir Walter Scott

"Please. Just let me explain. You don't understand. It wasn't how it looked," I said to Kate as she, Kiara, and Deirdre ignored me the entire way to school on Monday morning. I had left the house extra early so I wouldn't miss them getting off their bus outside the bank, but they were in no mood to speak to me. However, I was not giving up. Kate would have to talk to me sometime. Apparently the two-day cool off on Saturday and Sunday didn't help and she was still extremely heated.

I went to my desk, removed my coat and sat down. I didn't say a word to anyone. I hated it when people were mad or upset, especially with me. I had to find a way to make her understand that I didn't do anything wrong and I didn't intentionally hurt her. I would sit quietly and patiently in my seat for the first three classes of the day and force her to talk to me during break. If she refused to talk to me during break, I would try again at a lunch, and then continue trying until she at least heard me out. I glanced her way every couple minutes and saw her sulking over her desk. If by chance we made eye contact I would mouth, "I'm sorry" but she just stared at me sourly and then after a split second would diverted her eyes.

When the bell rang releasing the students for break, I followed her out of the room and stood behind her in line for the shop. I had lost my appetite because of the guilt. She bought a bottle

of water and then turned to head back to the classroom. She was surprised to see me blocking her way out of the cafeteria. As I opened my mouth to speak she pushed right by me, nudging my shoulder, forcing me out of her pathway. I shouted her name as I jogged after her down the hallway. Her skills at the silent treatment were impressive, and there was nothing I could do to make her talk to me.

During lunch I walked into the gym, where table were set up and girls sat in groups eating their lunches. In the corner of the gym, Kate, Kiara, Deirdre, Amy, Sinead, Mairead, and Colleen were talking and eating their lunches. The table went dead silent when they noticed me coming. They pretended to have great concentration on the food in front of them.

"Look I know you're all incredibly mad at me, but what harm will it do to just hear me out," I said hoping that explaining myself to the entire group would prove to be helpful. If the rest of them would listen, Kate was bound to follow along.

"No matter what you say or do, you still lied. I just can't believe you did this to Kate," Kiara said putting a comforting hand on Kate's back.

"Okay. I don't think you know how truly sorry I am. I shouldn't have lied to you, but I didn't want to hurt you.

"What do you think, I couldn't handle it or something? I'm not some emotionally unstable freak," she said, raising her voice and catching the attention of other girls at surrounding tables.

"I'm going to be one hundred percent straightforward with you right now. No lies. Just the truth, and I want you all to hear it," I began. "Declan likes me and I can't help that, so when you told me you liked him I was too afraid to tell you the truth. Unfortunately, my Uncle Jack likes Declan so much

he makes me go out with him, even though I don't like Declan in that way. Plus he hates Liam's father with a fiery passion and refuses to let me see him. Because Declan still likes me, he tried to kiss me and you just happened to see that. What you didn't see, because you ran away, was that I pushed him off of me. Declan and I are friends and that's all. I want nothing more out of our relationship. I am so sorry for lying because I never would intentionally hurt you. Your friendship means so much to me, and I hope you can forgive me." I noticed, when I was done, it had all come out in a big rush. I stood there silently for a few minutes hoping someone would respond. They sat processing what I had said. "Now you've heard my side of the story and if you're still mad, I understand." I walked away.

I sat in my seat for the rest of the day, feeling confident that my speech was persuasive. On my way out the door at the end of the day, I heard Kate call after me.

"I'm sorry for overreacting," she said.

"I'm sorry that I didn't tell you," I said. We smiled at each other, and walked together until she reached her bus and I continued on my way.

"Can I get you anything to drink?" I asked the party of five I had just seated.

"No, thank you," one man responded for all five of them.

"Okay, well, just so you know tonight's soup is tomato and basil," I said, realizing I had pronounced the two words as any native Irish would say them.

"Um, excuse me miss," the man said getting my attention. "What type of basil is it?" he said snickering to the other four. I had no idea what was funny and told him I would ask the chef. Aiden was also confused but told me to tell the man it was fresh basil. When I relayed the information back to the man and the other four guests, he continued to confound me.

"So it's not faulty, is it?" he replied slapping his knee in a fit of hysteria.

"No Sir, it is not," I responded, now walking away and feeling dense for not knowing what his mockery meant. He had obviously realized that I was American and sensed a need to make me feel small for that simple fact. After I took their orders and brought them to their seats, I delivered the soup. He continued to make comments all through the course and I knew soon I wouldn't be able to handle him. Carolyn and Catriona sensed my frustration and sent me into the kitchen to have a break. I tried my best to explain to Aiden what the man had been saying to me.

He began laughing and looked tremendously amused. "He was joking with you!" Aiden explained while still laughing at my naiveté for not knowing. "*Fawlty Towers* is an English program on the telly. The main character is named is Basil." He continued laughing as he tried to imagine my confused facial expression when the man asked me such an absurd question. I felt embarrassed for the rest of the night and purposely avoided their table.

Toward the end of the evening Eugene came into the restaurant to make sure things was running smoothly.

"All is well," I assured him.

"Good to hear," he said. I was standing behind the bar polishing glasses and silverware that was freshly washed.

"You missed a spot," he said observing one of the glasses I had just finished.

"Thanks," I said getting annoyed that he was still watching over me. "You remember that I can't work on Saturday night or Sunday afternoon right?"

"And why not?" he asked, as if it was an outrageous request.

"I'm going to Dublin. That's the whole reason I started working here in the first place," I reminded him.

"Oh! Right. Don't forget, I'm getting old. That's fine, have a good time and be safe."

"Thanks," I said once again as he disappeared through the door and back into the kitchen.

At eight a.m. Saturday morning, I had already packed my bag and was ready to meet the girls at the train station to catch the nine o'clock to Dublin. However, something didn't feel right. I was missing something. A part of me felt naked, but I couldn't figure out what exactly was gone. Finally I realized. The claddagh ring my father had bought me for my twelfth birthday was missing from my right hand ring finger. I searched under the beds, inside all the drawers, in the sitting room, in the kitchen, and even in the bathroom but couldn't find the ring anywhere. It was reaching eight-thirty and I was on the verge of having a panic attack. I considered the one last place it could possibly be: the restaurant. Maybe it fell off while I was washing the dishes the night before. I said goodbye to Jack and Una and raced out the door lugging my bag of clothes along with me. I searched the restaurant high and low, but left without my ring. I went up to the house to ask Biddy if she had seen it. After that I would have to give up. She sat in her usual spot, still in her nightgown, sipping a

cup of tea and eating a slice of toast. I thrust open the door, startling Biddy.

"Jesus Christ. You scared the living daylights out of me, child!" she said holding her hand to her heart, making sure it was still beating.

"Sorry, I just… I lost my ring," I said as I hustled through the kitchen looking on the windowsills, in the cupboards, and on the floor.

"What are you looking for?" she asked in utter confusion.

"My claddagh ring. I lost it. Have you seen it? I love it and I never take it off and I don't see how it is possible that it's missing from my finger," I explained with rising hysteria in my voice. She started mumbling to herself.

"You didn't lose it my dear. I betcha the fairies took it," she said.

"And you accused Jack of being off his knob?" I said under my breath in response to the absurd idea she had conjured from her head.

"You asked for help and it's a greater force that's come to help you through your complicated time. The fairies will help you. I know it. They just needed something in return until the deed is done my dear."

"So they took something *this* important to me?" I asked amazed that I was starting to believe the illogical as a logical explanation for the missing ring.

I looked up and noticed the time.

"Oh no! I'm going to miss my train!" I shouted. "Bye Biddy. Thanks for your help." I raced out the door and back towards the train station that I had passed on my way to the restaurant.

I ran the entire way there. The girls stood with their moms, impatiently waiting for me.

"Sorry I'm late!" I said, running toward them. They kissed their moms goodbye and we boarded the train. Their mothers stood and waved to us as the train started the two-hour journey to Dublin. For the first time in a while, I missed my mother. I missed the kiss she gave me every night before I went to bed, and the smile she gave me every morning when I woke up. The girls soon took my mind off home when they began to delight me with the image of Dublin.

"This is going to be so much fun!" Kate yelped. The woman reading the newspaper across the aisle gave her a disgruntled look and then continued reading.

I stepped off the train last, following behind Deirdre. The train station was alive. It was in full commotion as all sorts of people moved on and off the multitude of trains. We continued through the station and out the doors where Kiara's aunt would be waiting to collect us. I walked through the automatic doors and the sun shone brightly in my eyes, blinding me from my first vision of the city. I could hear horns honking, taxis weaving in and out of traffic, and a bus engine starting up, ready to take its passengers to different locations. Finally, I could see where I walked as we entered the shadow of a tall building. Kiara had already run over to where her aunt was standing, leaning against her car.

"Hello! You must be Sarah. It's great to meet you. Welcome to Dublin," she said, holding out her arms as if she was inviting me into her home and allowing me to embrace the spectacular place. We drove through terrible traffic for about twenty minutes and didn't get very far. Finally we left the

noise and hustle behind and arrived at a little area with endless rows of quaint townhouses. Kiara's Aunt Peggy showed the four of us inside and we set our bags in the room she provided.

"It's not much, but it's home, right?" Peggy said, looking around her house.

"It's very nice," I replied.

"Would you like some tea, girls?"

"No, we're all right," Kiara, said answering for all of us. "We really want to show Sarah the town. Can we go out for a while?"

"Oh go ahead. Be careful and don't get lost. Be home around four because your uncle and cousin will be back then and I'm making a dinner," she said as we raced to get our purses, step out into the sun and welcome the day ahead of us.

We were headed toward the center of Dublin: St. Stephen's Green, a twenty-seven acre park in the heart of Dublin. People were hustling about through the streets, heading to work, shopping, and eating. I couldn't believe the difference between Thurles and Dublin, and I had only been there twenty minutes. We soon arrived on Grafton Street, where the excitement really began.

"This is amazing," I said as I slowly walked down the street with them, taking in every sight. It was like the New York City of Ireland. There were people from many different countries, which was different from the solely Irish population that made up the overwhelming majority of Thurles. The street was blocked off and cars could not drive on it. The girls told me that thousands of people walked Grafton Street every day. There were musicians playing instruments for money, and they greeted you with kindness and appreciated all that anyone cared to donate. There were people doing tricks from juggling

to magic and showing off their various talents. The street was also filled with dozens of clothing stores. The four of us were definitely prepared to browse and buy.

"I love Dublin," Kate exclaimed elatedly. The rest of us agreed. It was like being in another land. Even the accent was different from Thurles. I was the foreigner in Thurles, but here in Dublin, we all felt different. I had been to large cities before, but there was something extra about the experience; the possibilities seemed endless.

We entered a store called Penneys. It is similar to a department store, like H&M, filled with everything you would need, from sunglasses, to underwear, to jeans. We eagerly went inside and began trying on clothes. Whenever we each had an outfit on we shouted, "out" and came out of our dressing rooms dancing and acting like models in front of the three-way mirrors, bopping to the upbeat pop music that was being played throughout the store. I bought a skirt as the weather was getting warmer, and a couple of shirts. We shopped for a while more and then stopped at a coffee shop to sit and take a break. Afterward we walked a couple of blocks over to Nassau Street to look around in the many Irish craft shops. I found presents to bring home to my family and a present for both Jack and Una. I also found presents for each of my friends back home in America. I bought Sophie a beautiful wool scarf that I knew she would appreciate during the cold and snowy Syracuse winters. I bought Hailey an Irish T-shirt that had an inappropriate saying on it, and for Taylor a necklace with a Celtic symbol on it. I had spent nearly all of the previous week's pay check.

It was reaching three o'clock when we entered Stephen's Green to sit down and relax for a bit.

"Thanks so much for asking me to come. I'm having so much fun already," I told Kiara. "It feels like all my confusion is gone since I arrived."

"I'm glad," she said. We sat in the Green for a while, keeping our eyes peeled for good-looking Dubliners.

On our way back to Peggy's house, we passed a neat little jewelry shop. In the window were various claddagh rings. I stopped to look, thinking again about what had happened to mine.

"They are gorgeous, aren't they," Deirdre said noticing me eyeing the rings in the window. "Loads of people wear them here, you should get one."

"I had one that my father gave me, but it's gone missing," I said sounding distressed.

"Go in and buy one!" Kate suggested. I opened the door to the shop and asked to try one on. I chose a simple sterling silver one, almost identical to the one I had lost, or maybe misplaced.

"It's lovely," Kate crooned. With the ring back on my finger, my hand felt much better. "Oops," she said.

"What?" She took the ring off my finger and turned it right side up so the hands were pointing toward me.

"Your heart's taken, remember?" she said, smiling at me.

"Table for one please," I said walking back into the restaurant around three o'clock the next day. The restaurant was near closing, but I wanted to find Aisling and Grainne before going home.

"Oh, Hey!" Grainne said. "How was Dublin?"

"It was a blast. I loved it."

"Good, good. Do you want some dinner? I'll have Aiden make you something."

"Yea, actually I'm starved, thanks." As Grainne went through one door into the kitchen to put my order in, Aisling came out the other.

"Hey sweetie pie!" she said giving me a big hug. "We missed you. How was Dublin?"

"It was great. We went shopping and Kiara's aunt was very nice and everything."

I sat alone and ate my Sunday lunch of turkey, mashed potatoes, and carrots in peace, watching the horses graze in the field behind the restaurant. Grainne or Aisling frequently swung by the table to talk to me. After the restaurant closed I helped them finish cleaning up and we walked home together.

That night Grainne and Aisling headed out on the town. I rented a movie and watched it while I lay in bed, trying to fall asleep. It had been two days since I had seen Liam, but it had felt much longer than that. I couldn't stop thinking about him and I wanted to fall asleep instantly so I could see him in my dreams.

"Is everyone getting prepared to go camping?" Miss Dwyer said immediately after we finished saying our morning prayer. "It's coming up, you know?" Each of us responded with a nod of our heads. "We aren't going to be sleeping in tents, so you'll need a sleeping bag of some sort. If you don't have one, borrow one from a friend. If you don't have any of those, then

you're out of luck! I've written up an itinerary and a list of items each of you should bring. Look over the lists and if you have any questions throughout the week, I'll be in my office." She left the room and a substitute came in. She advised us to review the papers Miss Dwyer had provided and then said we could do anything as long as we kept quiet. I put my papers in my bag to look at later at home. I went and sat in the vacant desk next to Kiara. We re-capped on the events of the weekend and talked about the upcoming class camping trip.

At the end of the day I sat under the tree and read over the camping trip itinerary while I waited for Liam to arrive.

Trip Itinerary

9:00 a.m. – Meet outside school to board bus

9:30 a.m. – Arrive at the Devil's Bit

10:00 a.m. – Hike up the Devil's Bit

12:30 p.m. – Stop to eat lunch

3:00 p.m. – Arrive at the top

4:00 p.m. – Head down to the camp site

5:00 p.m. – Swim

6:00 p.m. – Dinner

7:30 p.m. – Games

9:00 p.m. – Stories by the campfire

10:30 p.m. – Bed

Don't forget to bring:

Flashlight, sleeping bag, pillow, sweatshirt, bathing suit, change of clothes, towel, toothbrush, lots of water and good hiking shoes!

Before I even read "what not to forget to bring", someone snatched the paper right from my hands. I turned around and Liam was standing there reading it over, with a giant smile on his face.

"Hey you! Give me that!" I said, snatching it back from him. He scooped me up into his arms.

"I missed you," he said with excitement in his voice. "I'm never letting you go."

"Do you want to walk down to my granny's with me? I'll introduce you to everyone?"

He hesitated. A nervous look flashed over his face. "I won't be offended if you say no," I assured him.

"Sure, why not?," he said after a couple minutes of thought. "Your family couldn't be much worse than my own."

I laughed and grabbed his hand. As we walked toward Biddy's house other kids who had just gotten out of school were in and out of shops. About a hundred yards away I saw a man riding his bike toward Liam and I. As he came closer I realized it was Jack. I quickly grabbed Liam's hand and pulled him around the the shop we were walking past.

"Did he see us?" I asked nervously.

"Did who see us?" Liam asked.

"Jack. Did Jack see us?" I verified. "He just rode past us on his bike."

"Oh, I didn't even see him. Who cares if he saw us?" Liam asked.

"I do!" I exclaimed. "Remember we aren't supposed to see each other."

"You actually agreed not to see me?" Liam asked sounding extremely offended.

I realized that I made him feel bad.

"I'm sorry. It's just."

"It's just what Sarah?" he asked getting frustrated with me. I wasn't prepared to get in a fight with him.

"I'm sorry. I'll talk to him. I promise," I assured him. "Don't be mad at me, please," I said giving him sincere puppy eyes. He smiled and we held hands the rest of the way to Biddy's. Nonetheless, I kept a good eye out for men zooming past on their bikes.

We walked up the driveway and Paul, James, Eoghan, and Bill were passing the rugby ball around. Mary was in the arena with Nora, Eimear and Joe were in the sitting room, and Biddy was sitting contented, sipping a cup of tea, in her corner seat at the kitchen table. James threw the ball at me and I caught it and watched it spiral through the air as I quickly passed it to Liam, just as Paul had taught me. We played an extreme session of passing the ball around before I became exhausted, much sooner than the five of them. I walked, panting into the kitchen and grabbed a glass of water.

"Hey, Biddy," I said in between breaths.

"Well, Sarah?," she said.

"I was just outside passing around the rugby ball with the lads. Liam is out there as well," I told her sitting down to catch my breath.

"You tell him he better not skip off before I get a chance to meet him," she said sarcastically, although I sensed some sincerity in her voice. I laughed and assured her he would come in and introduce himself. After they were finished playing rugby, Mary and Nora also came up from the arena and into the house. Biddy went into cupboard and took out a cake she had made that morning. Bill, James, Paul, Eoghan, and Liam came in and sat down.

"Mary, Biddy. This is Liam," I said. He shook Mary and Biddy's hands. There was an awkward silence before everyone started babbling away again.

"Who wants tea?" Mary asked the entire room.

"Do you want a slice of cake, Liam?" Biddy asked. Within minutes, Joe and Eimear came in from the sitting room, and Eugene and Pat came up from the shop. The kitchen was packed with people as we drank tea, ate cake, and my family drilled Liam. I stood back and watched him tell all about himself and his family and observed the way my Uncles, Aunts, and Cousins took to him. Biddy was soon deep into conversation with him.

"So my class is going camping at the Devil's Bit," I said after the conversation stopped revolving around Liam.

"Oh, really? That's great!," Eugene said.

"What are you doing that for?" Eoghan asked.

"We're going to hike to the top, sleep outside, and tell stories around a fire," I explained to everyone.

"Watch out for the fairies up there," Biddy began. "They will mix things up. They always do. Don't go exploring alone either, Sarah. I'm warning you."

Mary helped Biddy out of her chair and brought her into the sitting room. "All right, let's go," Mary said. There was an awkward silence and soon everyone stood up from their seats and began to head back to their houses. Liam walked me most of the way home (so Jack wouldn't see him) and went to the square to catch the six thirty bus home.

I went in through the back door humming a merry tune and was stopped short by a disgruntled Jack.

"I thought I told you to stay away from that boy," he said angrily.

"You can't keep me from seeing him Jack!" I snapped back at him. I ran out of the room and up to my bed to sulk.

"My house, my rules," he shouted after me.

The rest of the week went by slowly. I worked Wednesday through Sunday and then another week began, only differently from prior weeks. The classroom buzzed as we all became more and more excited about the camping trip on Saturday.

Chapter 14

"Let's sing a song!" Kiara yelled to the rest of us in the bus.

"How about *I'll tell Me Ma"*?" suggested Kate.

"I think I know this one!" I told them. "My father used to sing it to me."

"*I'll tell me ma, when I go home, the boys won't leave the girls alone*," everyone sang, standing up from their seats:

They pull my hair, they stole my comb, and that's all right till I go home.

She is handsome, she is pretty, she is the belle of Belfast city, she is courtin' one, two, three, please won't you tell me who is she?

Albert Mooney says he loves her, all the boys are fighting for her. They knock at the door and they ring at the bell,

Sayin' 'Oh my true-love, are you well?'

I let the girls continue singing as I paused a moment to realize how much the song related to my life. I listened as they sustained the song.

Out she comes as white as snow, rings on her fingers, bells on her toes, Old Johnny Murray says she'll die, if she doesn't get the fellow with the roving eye.

I laughed at myself, because I in fact had a roving eye. It was strange how I had known this song my whole life and now it somewhat paralleled my situation.

Let the wind and rain and the hail blow high, and the snow come tumblin' from the sky. She's as sweet as apple pie, and she'll get her own lad by and by.

When she gets a lad of her own, she won't tell her ma when she gets home. Let them all come, as they will, for it's Albert Mooney she loves still," we sang breathlessly finishing the song.

The end of the song reminded my of Jack and how although I'm going to be with Liam no matter what, I had to hid it from him.

"Teach us an American song to sing this time!" Colleen cried from the front of the bus. I thought for a couple minutes and came up with a song that I knew they wouldn't recognize.

"Okay, here's one," I began to explain. "Whenever I say 'When she comes' you repeat it after me following the beat."

"Okay," they responded, seeming very eager to hear the song.

"*She'll be comin' round the mountain, when she comes*," I sang.

"*When she comes*," they echoed back to me.

"*She'll be comin' round the mountain, when she comes.*"

"*When she comes.*"

"*She'll be comin' round the mountain, she'll be comin' round the mountain, she'll be comin' round the mountain, when she comes.*"

"*When she comes.*"

I taught them all the verses and they were pleased to learn such an American sounding song.

"Woo!" I shouted, applauding them hastily.

"All right ladies. We're here!" Miss Dwyer said. Everyone on the bus jumped up from her seat eagerly.

As we filed off thc bus Miss Dwyer told us that our bags would be taken up to the campsite, and we would be walking to the top. We looked upward in horror, using our hands to shield our eyes from the brightness of the sun. All the way at the top I saw a white cross, which from the bottom was the size of my pinky finger.

The first part of the hike seemed easy enough as we began to maneuver the Bit by walking through a field. After some time we stopped at a flat area. I scanned the rest of the way to the top. My mouth dropped. The beginning had been rather deceiving. The rest of the way we would be tackling steep hills and rocky cliffs. As everyone continued to walk I whispered something in Kate's ear.

"I have to take a piss. What do I do?"

"I have to go as well!" she said. I scanned the area. The forest started a few yards from where we were standing. While Miss Dwyer was at the head of the group explaining about some type of plant, Kate and I snuck off. We each chose an appropriate size tree to hide behind, about one hundred yards away from the group, quickly did our business, and slipped back into the bunch of girls as we continued upward.

Finally, once we reached the top, I took in a deep breath of fresh air and looked out at the view. It was nothing spectacular, but it gave you a sense of accomplishment. The pain of the hike was finally over. There were houses and farms in the distance, and it seemed as though the sky went on for miles. I stood in front of the cross taking in everything that I could. The cross appeared to be much larger than I had expected from my miniscule view from the bottom. It was covered in signatures and notes left behind by people who had

also reached the top in the past. The wind blew strong as the entire class stood in a line at the edge of the cliff, our hair blowing in every direction, and we were silent for some time. Up there, there was time to think. There was peace. Miss Dwyer directed us to begin our descent down the hill a little ways toward the camp site. We arrived at a clearing in the forest where our bags had been piled into a big heap. There was a large grassy area where I assumed we would be sleeping, a small wooden hut, two picnic tables, and a large tree with a tire swing hanging from its branch. I immediately ran to it and hopped on. Deirdre followed and began to push me, as Miss Dwyer made sure we were all there. As I swung I noticed a little dirt pathway leading a bit deeper into the woods. While Miss Dwyer was counting, and re-counting us, Deirdre and I moved away and followed the path. It led to a small pond; one definitely big enough for twenty five girls to jump in. Deirdre and I looked at each other with exactly the same thought in our minds and ran back toward the group. Soon after we had persuaded Miss Dwyer, we were all suited up in swimwear and ready to cool off from our hike. Even Miss Dwyer dipped her feet in. After an hour of splashing, laughing, playing and cool-off time we dried and prepared to eat dinner. We had salad and sandwiches for dinner because there was no place to cook any food. After dinner, we thoroughly cleaned up hoping to avoid any hungry animals during the night. By this time it was nearly eight o'clock. We played two rounds of hide-and-go-seek and were finally tired and ready to settle down. We walked down another dirt path, one I hadn't noticed earlier. There was a dust pit and benches to sit on. Miss Dwyer ordered us to pair up and search for firewood.

"Make sure the wood is dry, and get pieces of all sizes!" Miss Dwyer called after the pairs of girls walking off in different directions.

"Ooo! Jackpot!" I said, catching Deidre's attention. I had found a perfect pile of wood for the fire.

"It looks like a little hut or something," I said, noticing the strange way the wood was already arranged. I picked up a piece to confirm that it was dry. Instantly I discovered a glowing light that was flying about frantically. It began to pester me, flying circles around my head. I looked closer at the insect like figure which was quite peculiar.

"Deidre, do you know what this is?" I said sounding shocked.

"I think it's a lightning bug," she said.

"I don't think so, Deirdre," I replied, keeping my eyes on the weird light.

Miss Dwyer called us back to the fire pit and Deirdre ran off, leaving me standing there still marveling over the creature.

"You are definitely not a lightning bug," I said while I examined its sparkling wings and the magical glow that formed a halo around it. I put the piece of wood back down and ran toward the rest of the girls.

The fire was crackling as we all sat comfortably around it, warming our hands and feet in the chill of the night. When we were all settled we began to share stories. Miss Dwyer scared us with the stories of the Banshee and intrigued us with the mysterious adventures of the Dullahan. The fire, still burning bright, left a daunting glare on her face as she spoke to us in a deep and chilling voice. Afterward we decided to lighten the mood by singing a few songs, including *Rocky Road To Dublin*, *Danny Boy*, and a song sang in Gaelic. I daringly sang for entire group *The Star Spangled Banner*, and *This Land is your Land*. They were all impressed by my singing ability but by the end I was red with embarrassment. By now it was dark and surely they couldn't see my face. By nine thirty, after

another two stories, I noticed all the girls were either yawning or half asleep.

When we all climbed into our sleeping bags it was inevitable that we would group off. I lay down next to Maread and was surrounded by Kate, Kiara, Amy, Sinead, and Deirdre. We rested our chins in the palms of our hands and talked for a while.

"How are things with Liam, Sarah?" Amy asked.

"Things are fine. I guess. I think I'm really falling for him but I know deep down I shouldn't. I have to leave here in a month. It's so weird. Five months ago I left my family, my friends, my entire culture and now I'm going back. I don't even feel that I've had enough time with my Irish relations. I guess I never realized how much change I would go through here, and soon I'm going to have to go back to my old life. Not to mention leaving all of you. You befriended me when I came and I'll never forget that. You've listened to me during the good and the ba-."

Suddenly I noticed a strange silence. I looked around, only to realize that everyone else was sound asleep. I had been talking to myself for who knows how long. I laughed at my ability to ramble on.

It felt like it had been an hour but in fact it had been only three minutes. I couldn't fall asleep. I lay there with my eyes wide open staring at the sky. I tried counting sheep but, lost count. I tried counting stars but there were too many, and I tried singing myself to sleep but I only ended up waking a few grumpy and sleepy campers. The stars were amazing. I couldn't take my eyes off them. They glistened like diamonds in the sky. I tossed and turned in my sleeping bag. I didn't know whether it was the hard ground and unfamiliar place or whether I was simply restless and keyed up. I slowly unzipped

my sleeping bag, put my jeans and sweatshirt back on, grabbed my flashlight, and headed toward the forest. When I was finally a fair distance from my classmates I turned the flashlight back on and began to sing to myself again, as I walked along.

"You got time and streets making saints and sinners, because she's making losers from winners. It's not what your dreams will be..."

It appeared to be much darker now because the trees' long thick branches kept the light of the moon from shining through their leaves. The trees swaying in the wind, animals scurrying about, and the consistent "woo" of an owl sent chills through my body. I was beginning to think walking off on my own was a bad idea. I turned around to head back toward the group and saw a light glowing up in a tree. I inched closer in hopes of getting a better look but it flew around, from tree to tree, making it difficult for my eyes to follow it. I tried to keep focused on the light as it soared through the air, spinning around my head. It blurred my vision and suddenly it disappeared again, only this time for good. I turned to go back and realized that following the light had brought me some place I didn't recognize. I circled around looking for something familiar but knew nothing. My lip began to quiver as my knees became weak and I fell to the ground. I heard the voice of one of the girls from the campsite. I recognized the voice to be Kate's and figured she would see that I had gone, and would come looking for me.

I saw a faint beam of light, and assumed that Kate had turned her flashlight on and would follow my footsteps into the woods.

Suddenly the sparkle of light from before appeared and began to swerve around my head, going faster each second. I began feeling dizzy as my head hit the hard ground and I instantly

feel asleep. I desperately tried to stay awake so I could shout for Kate to come find me, but this small and unusual speck of light gave me no choice.

I had no recollection of time of place when I awoke from my unconscious state. As I gained balance and stood up from the cold, dry pile of leaves that I had been sleeping on top of, I tried to find my way back toward the campsite; the only safe, comfortable place nearby.

Now, amidst a sparkling night sky I wandered, trying to find my way, as Kate, who I suspected was somewhere within the forest, tried to make her way through the trees by the glistening moonlight.

Come fairies
Take me out of this dull world,
For I would ride with you
Upon the wind and dance
Upon the mountains like a flame.

-W.B. Yeats

Chapter 15

I must have traveled in the complete opposite way of the campsite and all my sleeping classmates because I came to a clearing where I suddenly became very shocked and confused.

Before my very eyes stood Declan, Liam and Kate. The flicker of light was spinning around them hastily. However surreal, it had entranced them with its vibrant colors and graceful movements and I stood in awe watching it engross them. It flipped, dove, and flew in every which direction forcing them to spin around. Sparks of light flew from the miraculous creature's body as it landed upon their heads. After twenty or so minutes of hectic swirling, the beautiful winged creature became quieter, and Declan, Liam and Kate slowly fell to the ground.

They lay there serenely as the creature looked over them with a look of accomplishment. I ran to them as the light swiftly flew out of sight, and shook them intensely, desperately trying to wake them. However, they just lay there, peacefully sleeping.

I was bewildered and stunned to see them there. I had no idea where Liam and Declan had come from, when they had arrived, or how they had gotten here. I sat down under a tree across from where the three of them lay and waited for the time when they snapped out of their haze, as all of them would have an extreme amount of explaining to do. As I sat there watching them, my eyes grew heavy and my body weak. I was tired from walking and leaned against the tree and fell asleep.

* * *

Still, with no recollection of time or place, I woke to a noisy fit of discussion. I opened my eyes to see that Kate, Declan, and Liam had woken up.

Kate looked extremely perplexed, and Declan and Liam still appeared to be in a trance. They barely noticed me there in their hysterical conversation and I listened closely to get a clue.

"Am I dreaming?" Kate said loudly. She appeared to be very distressed.

"Am I?" Declan and Liam said at the same time looking dreamily into Kate's eyes.

"I have never seen anything as beautiful as you," Liam said, reaching out to hold her hand. He slowly lifted it to his lips but Kate quickly snatched it back. She turned to Declan.

"I could gaze into your gorgeous eyes forever," he said completely mesmerized by her features. Kate stood up and faced the two boys, both of them staring at her like they were lost puppies.

"Liam! Kate! Declan!" I said in utter excitement. The three of them immediately stopped talking and faced me. "What is going on?" I asked, after seeing this ridiculous dialogue going on before me.

"I love Kate," Declan said, bluntly.

"I love Kate," Liam said, staring at Declan with cruel eyes.

I looked at Kate, but she was just as confused as I was. I searched Liam's eyes for laughter, hoping that this was just a joke, but I only found seriousness.

He turned to me. "I'm sorry, Sarah," he said, staring at the ground and looking ashamed. He then looked up and took Kate's hands in his. "I love you, Kate."

Declan rapidly butted in. "I saw her first." He snatched Kate's hands and softly caressed them. "I love you Kate."

"What is going on? This isn't funny!" Kate cried in astonishment.

"I agree!" I shouted.

I stood there in shock, watching the boy I loved tell me he loved my friend. Tears rolled down my face and hit the ground callously.

"This isn't a joke, my dearest," Liam said, looking at Kate with wistful eyes. He was practically drooling over her. I didn't understand. What had happened here? Had I done something wrong? Kate turned to walk away but stopped short. She turned back toward the three of us who were still standing there to say one last thing.

"This is a cruel and horrible joke to play on me!" she cried. Declan and Liam hurried after her as she ran off into the distance. I stood there alone watching Liam run out of my life. I was mystified. My lingering confusion told me that something just wasn't right. I knew something had happened and I was determined to find out. I ran off in the direction of Kate, Declan, and Liam in the hope of catching up with them.

When I finally reached them they were standing in another, but different, clearing under the trees. Declan was pulling Kate's arm toward him, and Liam was pulling her other arm in the opposite direction. Kate was still crying now, somewhat out of physical pain, but mostly out of emotional pain.

"I don't understand. What's happening Liam?" I shouted over Kate's shrill screams.

"I really don't know, Sarah. I just know that I don't love you anymore," he said still staring at Kate. I stared coldly at Kate.

"What did you do Kate?" I yelled at her in absolute anger. I was bitter and hurt and hysterical. I sat down and put my face in my hands. Kate somehow managed to free herself from the two vultures and ran away again. I heard her screaming as she ran.

"I don't want either of you! Just leave me alone!" I heard Kate yell.

I lifted my face from my hands. I was alone-very alone. More alone than I had ever felt in my entire life. It was dark and cold, and now the scary forest noises that had always been there, had turned into startling and spooky sounds. I wrapped my hands around my body and shivered. I couldn't move. I was lost and had nobody and nowhere to go.

I thought for a long while about what could have happened. After a long while of sulking, I stood up.

"There's magic in this forest. I know it. How else can you explain this?" I said to myself feeling upbeat and certain of the fact. I began walking in the direction where Kate, Liam and Declan had run. I picked up pace, running then sprinting toward where I thought they had gone. I had left my flashlight behind and it was very dark, but I was determined to find them and fix this unusual, romantic, tangle.

As I ran, the light appeared by my side, almost as if it was guiding me. It whisked through the forest dodging branches left and right. Anxiously, it glistened above me and although I was breathlessly panting, I heard a faint whisper.

"I will put back what I have done, so the four lovers will love the right one."

I smiled as we moved together as I knew this amazing creature was going to help me.

"As I tried to make better, what I only made worse, I must quickly find them to change love's curse."

I heard thc sound of Kate's hysteria as we came closer to Declan, Liam and her.

When we reached them we stood silently, as the four of us watched the light, completely enchanted.

The fairy was now ready to amend what she had done. She flew around us chanting in a quiet murmur.

It planted a kiss on each one of our heads as we drifted off into dreamland. It flew off instantly into the starry night's sky.

As the sun slowly rose over the Devil's Bit, an orchestra of creatures awoke. Each one sang, buzzed, or hummed their morning tune. Foggy morning dew formed on the tree leaves, as the warmth of the sun made the cold nights chill disappear. The sun's bright light peeked through the breaks in the tree branches, flooding the clearing with creamy, yellow warmth. I awoke in the comfort of Liam's arms. I smiled at him as I watched him still sleeping, the movements of his chest rising and falling. I touched his shoulder to wake him and he opened his eyes wide and smiled down at me.

"I could wake up to your gorgeous eyes everyday, no problem," he said pulling me closer and squeezing me tight.

We looked over toward the Kate and Declan. Declan was holding Kate, just as Liam had been holding me. They were awake and smiling at one another.

The four of us looked around, trying to remember how we'd arrived to this unfamiliar place and where we were, but none of us could recall.

Declan and Kate, and Liam and I, shared our first kiss beneath the magical trees of the incredibly enchanted forest. We were interrupted by the noise of our classmates awaking nearby and remembered we had to get back before the Miss Dwyer noticed we were missing.

"How are we going to explain this to them?" I asked looking at Kate in bewilderment. There were no words or any reality for that matter to explain what had happened. Confusion struck the forest, leading us all into the disorder. After a passionate goodbye, we watched the boys head back out of the forest and smiled to ourselves.

"I don't think I've ever felt this perplexed, but genuinely blissful at the same time," Kate said to me. We went arm and arm back to our classmates, to find some way to explain last night. However, even if we could explain, would they ever believe us?

Chapter 16

We ran toward the noises of our classmates waking up to the morning sun.

"Hey, Kate and Sarah are missing!" I heard Colleen's voice roar.

"Ooo, they're going to be in trouble!" Maeve screeched along with her.

Kate and I looked at each other in fear of what Miss Dwyer was going to do to us. When we reached the campsite everyone was silent. They stared at Kate and me with dark eyes that shot through my body like a bullet. Miss Dwyer stood in front of them tall and stern.

"Where have the two of you been?" she asked crossly. "You can't just wander off like that. Do you have any idea how dangerous that was?"

Her lip was twitching as she yelled at us and I couldn't help but laugh inside. She had her hand on her hip and had stuck her wagging finger so close to my face it was almost touching my nose.

"You think this is funny, don't you?" she asked seriously.

"No Miss. I don't think this is funny," Kate said, switching over to teacher's pet mode.

"Miss Dwyer, please let us explain," I said hoping she would agree to hear me out.

"You have an awful lot of explaining to do," she said with her lip still twitching frantically. Then the twitching stopped and she planted a sly grin on her face.

"I think you should wait though. You can explain it to me and Principal Mulroney first thing tomorrow morning."

Kate and I looked at each other in fear. When Miss Dwyer got angry her lip twitched and it was bad enough, but when Miss Mulroney got mad, her entire body twitched and she spat all over you. I dreaded having to explain what happened, especially sense I had no idea, but at least I had the bus ride back to school to make up a complex, and believable lie.

"Come along girls, let's make our way back down," Miss Dwyer said as she began rolling her sleeping bag up and precisely counting how many girls were present.

The walk down the Devil's Bit was the longest awkward silence I had ever experienced.

"Hey," Kiara whispered making her way over to where I was. "What happened last night?" she said, seeming intrigued.

"I'm honestly couldn't tell you. I walked off when I wouldn't sleep and then crazy and mysterious things happened," I said to her.

"Like what?" she said begging for more detail.

"I truthfully don't remember anything. I woke up under a tree in Liam's arms, and Kate was in Declan's."

Kiara gasped. "Oh! He was surprising you. How romantic," she said dreamily. "I'm still confused though."

"You're confused?" I asked sarcastically. "I do remember one thing though," I said. "I barely remember this creature; a little flicker of light really. It could fly. It did strange and unusual things. I honest to God think it was-" I leaned into her so I could whisper the next part in her ear.

"A fairy."

"You're delirious," she said laughing. She put her arm around me, satisfied with the fact that she would never understand.

"It's no use. They'll never believe us," I said looking over to Kate. She shrugged and kept walking.

The rest of the way down the hill we all stayed perfectly silent. Every time I looked over at Kiara she would chuckle but I just ignored her. The bus ride back to school was also silent, except for Kate and I trying to compile a story. Thankfully it was Sunday so we couldn't go straight into the school to get yelled at some more. We would have to wait for school the next morning when we could get called down to the office to get lectured. I was extremely tired from the walk down the bit and I couldn't wait to get home and into bed. I thankfully hitched a ride with Regina so didn't have to walk.

The house was silent. I searched every room but no one was home. I figured Grainne and Aisling were at work, but I had no idea where Una or Jack could be on a Sunday. It was kind of nice that I had the house to myself. I hadn't had much space or time of my own since I had come to live there and it was a pleasant change. I brought my things up to my room and threw them on the floor along with Aisling and Grainne's clothes that were scattered everywhere.

The last thing I remember was my head hitting the pillow.

I woke up to the sound of Aisling and Grainne rushing about the room packing their things to go back to college. I looked at the clock next to my bed. It read seven o'clock. Aisling threw the curtains open.

"Mornin' sunshine!" I moaned rolling over in my bed and hiding my face in my pillow.

"How are you this cheerful in the morning?" I asked her grumpily.

"Don't tell me you're still tired. You went to bed in the afternoon yesterday!" Grainne added.

"So how was the camping trip anyways?" Aisling asked. I didn't feel like explaining the whole story when I could hardly even recollect it myself. I decided on a simple answer to satisfy them and hope that they wouldn't ask questions.

"It was great," I told them getting out of bed and rushing to the bathroom to take a shower.

I dreaded walking into school. I met Kate outside the door and we decided to endure it together. Before we had taken our coats off, Miss Dwyer spotted us and demanded we follow her to Principal Mulroney's office.

There were two chairs placed directly in front of her desk and she ordered us to sit down. Miss Mulrouney did not look happy, and her body was already beginning to twitch with anxiety.

"I'll give you five minutes to explain yourselves," she said sternly.

Kate and I had decided ahead of time to go with the truth. We would explain as much of it as we could and accept the punishment together.

I started off by explaining how I couldn't fall asleep. I basically told her the story I told Kiara, with a few modifications. When I got to the part about the enchanting light, her eyes widened, but surprisingly, she didn't laugh. Miss Dwyer had a similar reaction.

"I honestly have a very blurred memory of what happened that night. I remember the light, and I remember waking up under a tree. All I know is that there was a whole lot of confusion in

that forest, but somehow everything ended up all right and I know nothing dangerous happened. It was very irresponsible for us to wander off and I'm sorry."

The four of us were silent for a while as Miss Mulroney and Miss Dwyer processed the information I had given to the best of my knowledge. I was nervous to hear their response. What if they thought I was on drugs or something? Miss Mulroney stood up from her seat and looked down at Kate and me.

"Girls, I don't know exactly what happened last night and I don't think we'll ever know for sure. This isn't the first time I have heard a story like the one you have told, however, you must realize that sleeping under the trees of the Devil's Bit, on a starry, moonlit night in the woods, can often lead to magical dreams."

Miss Dwyer opened the door to allow Kate and me to leave. She said nothing as we left the office. Kate and I looked at each other in complete and utter bewilderment and headed back to the room for our first class.

I assumed that Miss Mulroney had some understanding of what had happened because she was familiar with the ways of the Devil's Bit, and we took our "non-punishment" with relief.

The last week of school went by quickly, and as the weekend approached I was sad, because it was my last. I had three great nights out with my girls, Aisling and Grainne, and Liam. I was leaving Tuesday morning and spent all day Monday saying goodbye to people, getting presents for my mom and dad, stocking up on tons of Cadbury's chocolate, and packing.

Saying goodbye to Liam was something I had been dreading, although I'd been preparing myself since the day we had met. I was fully stocked with tissues and I had written him a letter to read after I was gone.

To Liam:

My six months in Thurles were amazing. I had some of the best times of my life here. I learned so much about myself and my past while living here and being around my family. I made friends that I know I will never lose and a first love I will never forget.

Love always, Sarah

p.s. Missing you already. See you at Christmas!

Tears welled up in my eyes as I re-read the letter to myself before placing it inside a crisp white envelope. I wrote "Liam" on the front, and carefully placed it inside my bag. We were meeting at eleven o'clock on Monday morning at our spot by the river where we often met after school. Out of nervousness I had arrived early and was sitting in my usual nook in the tree watching the water slowly pass. I remembered all the times I had spent with him. It would be so hard to leave. Only three minutes had passed and I heard him walking toward me. I stood up from the ground and turned around and smiled widely. The sight of him made me want to burst into tears despite my smile. He put his arms around me and we stood in silence for a while. We sat down and looked at the water. We had nothing to say to each other. It was almost awkward.

"I'm going to miss you," he said pulling out loose grass blades as he stared down at his hands.

I crawled toward him and pressed my lips up against his as tears began streaming down my face. I pulled away and he wiped my cheeks with the back of his finger.

"Don't cry. Please don't," he said begging me. I nodded okay. "You're beautiful," he told me. I looked up at him, my eyes

soggy with tears, my palms moist with sweat, and my nose dry from the weather. I smiled.

"I love you," I said quietly.

"I love you more," he said in return. I wiped the remaining tears off my face and searched inside my purse for the envelope. I handed it to him.

"Don't read it until I'm gone," I demanded. He put his arms around me once more and we sat holding each other. Then he let go and pointed at something that was under the tree.

"Is that you Claddah ring?" he asked curiously grabbing it from the grass.

"It can't be," I told him. I lost that ages ago," I insisted. He handed it to me and I looked at the inside rim where my father had it engraved.

It read "Sarah" on the band. I gasped in shock.

"I have no idea how this got here," I said, my eyes wide with surprise.

I thought of what Biddy had told me on the morning when I first discovered I had lost it. She was rambling on about fairies and how they had probably taken it when I needed help. Now that I no longer needed help, it had re-appeared. I remember thinking she was slightly delirious that morning, however, now I had a little more faith.

I lifted his hand and slid it right onto his pinky. "You don't actually have to wear it," I laughed, "but I want you to have it." To my alarm and disappointment he slid the ring right off his finger. Then he surprised me once more. He slid it back on his finger, only this time with the heart pointing toward him.

"I'm taken," he said looking up at me. My face grew red with excitement.

It took time to make myself get off the ground, and then more time to let go of his hand. He walked slowly away, then stopped and ran back to me. He kissed me and assured me

everything would be all right. When he really walked away I stood watching him get smaller and smaller as the distance grew between us. I cried when he turned the corner of a building and disappeared from sight.

I walked out into the town, where crowds of people were hustling about. I made my way across the street. I had asked Kiara, Kate, Sinead, Deirdre, Amy, and Mairead to meet me in 'our spot' in the back corner of the upper level of Hayes Hotel. We'd had a mass on the last night of school where we sang songs from our music class, and many of us gave speeches. I recited a beautiful reflection. I spoke the words from my heart to each girl in my class and the teachers. I was going home a changed girl for many reasons. I had grown and learned so much about myself. I had made new friends and met and became close with my family members. I would be going back to Syracuse a different person, and I wanted to make sure they knew I was grateful for their openness and willingness to befriend me, and I wanted to thank them for all their generosity when I first arrived.

"I just said goodbye to Liam," I told them.

"Aww," they all said in an exaggerated way. They hopped off their stools and hugged me at the same time.

We were all sad, and clearly exhausted.

"It feels like I just arrived yesterday," I said as my lips automatically turned down and formed my sad face.

"Time does fly by, doesn't it lads," Kiara said, their heads nodding in agreement.

Time does fly by, I thought. It was over. The story had ended and I was going home. No, I was going back to Syracuse. Here, in Ireland I had my heritage, my culture, and my true happiness. Now, Ireland was my home.